The secret to success . . .

"Three cheers for Jessica," Kimberly said, holding up her lemonade.

"Hip, hip, hooray!" the Unicorns cried.

Jessica sat back in her lounge chair, smiling with pleasure. She could definitely get used to this.

"Well," said Mandy Miller after the cheering had died down. "Now that we're all in it together, you can let us in on the secret ingredients. What did you put in your cookies to make them so delicious?"

The smile on Jessica's face faded a little. "The secret ingredients?"

"Extra vanilla?" Grace Oliver asked, her dark eyes shining.

"Chopped pecans?" Mary Wallace suggested.

"White chocolate?" Mandy put in.

Jessica cleared her throat. The secret ingredients. Right. The secret ingredients were . . . *She remembered that some stuff had fallen into her batter—but what had it been?*

SWEET VALLEY TWINS

Jessica's Cookie Disaster

Written by
Jamie Suzanne

Created by
FRANCINE PASCAL

BANTAM BOOKS
NEW YORK • TORONTO • LONDON • SYDNEY • AUCKLAND

RL 4, 008-012

JESSICA'S COOKIE DISASTER
A Bantam Book / August 1995

Sweet Valley High® and Sweet Valley Twins™ are registered trademarks of Francine Pascal

Conceived by Francine Pascal

Produced by Daniel Weiss Associates, Inc.
33 West 17th Street
New York, NY 10011

Cover art by James Mathewuse

ISBN: 0-553-48191-6

Published simultaneously in the United States and Canada

Bantam Books are published by Bantam Books, a division of Bantam Doubleday Dell Publishing Group, Inc. Its trademark, consisting of the words "Bantam Books" and the portrayal of a rooster, is Registered in the U.S. Patent and Trademark Office and in other countries. Marca Registrada. Bantam Books, 1540 Broadway, New York, New York 10036.

PRINTED IN THE UNITED STATES OF AMERICA

OPM 0 9 8 7 6 5 4 3 2 1

To Austin Diane Jacobson

One

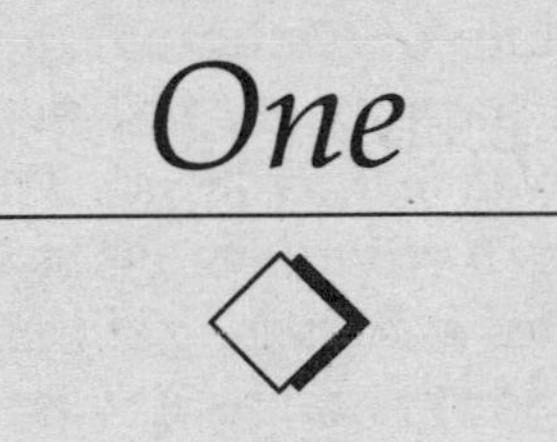

Click, click. Frowning with concentration, Jessica Wakefield slowly tapped the numbers into her calculator. She hit the equal sign, then blinked as the final number was displayed.

Three million, eight hundred thousand, sixty-eight.

She sighed. That couldn't be right.

It was a Monday afternoon, and Jessica was settled at the kitchen table with her after-school snack of Mallomars and a cold glass of milk. She took a thoughtful bite of cookie, then pushed the plate away.

"Three point two," she muttered, entering the figure again. "Two point nine . . ." She entered the rest of the numbers. "OK, now, add 'em up, divide by seven . . ."

"Yes!" She punched her fist into the air. It was as she had suspected. Because of that unexpected fluke of an A on her history test last week, Jessica was hovering on the edge of the honor roll for the first time in her life. She couldn't believe it. School to her was mainly a place to socialize with her friends, show off her latest outfits, and boy-watch. But somehow fate was intervening. Somehow her grades, almost with a will of their own, had inched toward the honor roll level. It was too good to be true.

Taking a big bite of Mallomar, Jessica grinned. *At last,* she thought happily. *At last the world will see me for my true self. Not just as Jessica Wakefield, one of the most popular and pretty girls of Sweet Valley Middle School, but as Jessica Wakefield, girl genius. All right!*

Jessica had to admit that as it was, she already had a lot going for her. After all, she was a member of the Unicorns, which was the most exclusive group of girls at Sweet Valley Middle School. She was also a Booster, and everyone knew how difficult it was to be picked for the Sweet Valley Middle School cheering squad. And it didn't hurt that she had long, shiny blond hair, blue-green eyes, and a dimple in her left cheek. But there was something missing.

Amazing grades. Jessica wanted to be respected for her brains on top of everything else. Being on the honor roll would do that.

There's also the matter of Elizabeth, Jessica thought, taking a sip of milk. Elizabeth was her identical twin sister. Usually being an identical twin was great, and Elizabeth was the best sister in the world. But people tended to divide the girls up unfairly, looking for differences, any differences, to make the two girls seem more individual. After all, they looked so much alike that when they were little they had worn name bracelets so people could tell them apart.

Now that they were getting older, Jessica was used

to being thought of as the stylish twin, the one with fabulous fashion flair, the exciting, unpredictable one. And Elizabeth . . . well, people thought of Elizabeth as the smart one, the one who did well in school, the reliable one. Not that she wasn't popular in her own way. She had tons of friends, and everyone knew they could rely on Elizabeth.

In some ways, Jessica thought, people seemed to take Elizabeth more seriously. They listened when she talked, they asked her advice, they trusted her.

The last time Jessica had given someone advice was when she told her best friend, Lila Fowler, to definitely wear her ankle-strap espadrilles with her linen sundress. Not that that kind of advice wasn't important, but Jessica wanted to be relied on for things besides her fashion sense.

And now that she was just a hop, skip, and a jump away from being on the honor roll, it looked as though she would be. Finally, everyone would know that she and Elizabeth had more in common than just fabulous Southern California good looks. People would be sorry they had underestimated Jessica.

I knew I had it in me. Jessica ate another Mallomar.

Humming to herself, Elizabeth pulled out her house key and let herself into the Wakefield home. There had been a long *Sixers* meeting after school, but they had gotten a lot accomplished. Elizabeth was proud to be the editor of the sixth-grade newspaper, and working on the *Sweet Valley Sixers* was one of her favorite things to do. She hoped to be a real investigative reporter for a real newspaper someday.

Inside, she tossed her backpack on the stairs, then headed into the kitchen. Her twin sister, Jessica, was sitting at the kitchen table, surrounded by cookies, milk, a notepad, a pen, and a . . . calculator?

"Jessica?" Elizabeth said in a concerned voice. She came over and felt her sister's forehead. "Are you all right? You know, that isn't a Walkman. It's a . . . a calculator."

Jessica gave her sister an exasperated look, brushing her hand away. "Ha ha. Very funny. Pardon me while I pick myself up off the floor."

Elizabeth grinned, sat down, and took a cookie. "Sorry. It's just that it's a little unusual to see you with a calculator on a beautiful, sunny afternoon." She took a bite of her cookie. "Or on a rainy morning. Or a cloudy evening. Or a—"

"OK," Jessica growled. "That's enough. For your information—"

"Oh, I get it." Elizabeth's face cleared. She quit teasing and got down to business. "They're having a twenty-percent-off sale at Valley Fashions at the mall. You want me to help you figure it out?" She pulled the calculator closer to her to demonstrate. "OK. Say you see a cute jumper for $24.99. Now, if it's twenty percent off, you take the $24.99, and then *times* it by point two zero—"

"Give me that!" Jessica snatched the calculator back, and Elizabeth looked up in surprise.

"What's wrong?" she asked. "Are you really doing homework?"

"No," Jessica said impatiently. "For your information, I was figuring out which class I need to bring my grade up in."

"Jessica!" Elizabeth whispered, feeling a twinge of worry. "You're not about to flunk out, are you?" She'd always dreaded this. She *knew* Jessica didn't take school seriously enough.

To her surprise, Jessica only rolled her eyes. "No! In fact, just the opposite. I've been trying to tell you—I'm only a few points away from making the honor roll this month. I was just seeing which of my classes I should pull my grade up in to make it. I think just one A on a pop quiz should do it."

"The honor roll?" Elizabeth asked in astonishment. Every month a student's grades were compiled, and everyone who had an average of over 3.5 was put on the honor roll. The list was always posted on the big bulletin board by the principal's office. "Really?" Elizabeth wrinkled her brow. "Are you . . . sure?"

"Yes," Jessica said with exaggerated patience. She pushed her calculations toward Elizabeth. "See for yourself."

Elizabeth examined Jessica's grade list. It was amazing, it was unbelievable, but there it was. It had probably been the A in P.E. that had really pulled her up.

"Wow," Elizabeth said with a smile, feeling a glow of happiness. "Jess, this is fabulous!" She toasted Jessica with a Mallomar, and her sister grinned at her.

"I know it might be a little hard to believe," Jessica said modestly.

"But it's terrific! I'm so happy for you. It'll be so much fun for both of us to be on it. We're the unbeatable Wakefield twins, right?"

"Right!" Jessica was beaming from ear to ear.

Elizabeth got up to get herself her own plate of cookies

and glass of milk. "Mom and Dad will be really happy, too. It looks as if you need just a few more points. Do you know what class you're going to focus on?"

Jessica shook her head. "Not yet. My lowest grade is in English, but that would also be the hardest one to bring up. I guess I'll try for something easier."

"Well, if you want me to help you with anything, just let me know," Elizabeth offered. She knew Jessica would do the same for her. "I could quiz you, or lend you my notes . . . anything you want." She picked up her cookies and milk and started to head for the family room.

"Thanks, Elizabeth, but I'm going to do it all myself," Jessica said with a dismissive wave of her hand. "I'm very smart, you know."

"Oh, OK. Suit yourself," Elizabeth said from the hall with a grin. Jessica might have been almost on the honor roll, but that didn't necessarily make her more humble.

For a few moments Jessica sat at the kitchen table, anticipating everyone's reaction when she made the honor roll. Her parents would be really happy—maybe they would even buy her a present or something. And now that she was so obviously smart, even her fourteen-year-old brother Steven would have to take her more seriously. He'd no longer be able to call her "the sister who didn't have enough sense to come in out of the rain." *This* sister could not only come in out of the rain, she could predict the weather and tell you what kind of clouds were forming in the south.

Jessica chuckled to herself. Her friends would be

impressed, too. None of the Unicorns really focused on being an academic wonder—there were too many other important things to worry about. But if Jessica suddenly revealed her awesome mental powers . . . well, how could it hurt? She might just become *the* most important Unicorn.

Jessica stretched lazily, relishing her daydreams. Then a quick glance at the clock showed that it was almost time for her favorite afternoon show, *Lifestyles of the French and Famous.* Actually, it was a cooking show, hosted by Chef Crêpe, but he had fabulous guest stars, and they always showed some incredible video about some gorgeous château in France. And now that Jessica was just beginning to recognize her raw brainpower, it was probably a good idea to expose herself to some multiculturalism.

Jessica jumped up and headed into the family room. Elizabeth was already in there, sitting on the couch, her snack on the coffee table in front of her. The remote was in her hand, and she was channel-surfing.

Jessica plopped down next to her. "Remote, please," she said, snapping her fingers.

"What?" Elizabeth looked up. "I'm about to watch an Amanda Howard interview. You know she's my favorite author."

"Well, it's four thirty," Jessica said. "Time for *Lifestyles of the French and Famous.* You know I always watch it."

"Sorry," Elizabeth said firmly. "You'll have to watch it upstairs on Mom and Dad's TV. I have dibs on this one."

"I can't," Jessica said. "Their TV is in the shop, being repaired, remember?"

"Well, it's not my fault Steven spilled a whole can of soda down the back of it," Elizabeth replied. "Look, you watch *Lifestyles* every day—it won't kill you to miss a day. But who knows when they'll rerun the Amanda Howard interview? I've been waiting for this for weeks."

"Eliz-a-beth," Jessica said, feeling a little irritated. "Come on, just give me the remote. I can't miss this show. Just yesterday they had Anne-Michelle as the guest star. Who knows who they'll have today?" Jessica reached across Elizabeth for the remote, but her sister held it out of reach.

"Who's Anne-Michelle?" Elizabeth asked calmly. "And why should I care?" Suddenly she leaned closer to the TV and clicked up the volume. Jessica watched in dismay as a TV interviewer introduced a short, rather plump woman with silky gray hair.

"Is that Amanda Howard?" Jessica asked disdainfully. "She doesn't even look like a mystery writer. More like someone who writes computer manuals."

"Shh!" Elizabeth said, waving at Jessica to be quiet.

Jessica glared at her. Elizabeth wasn't trying to see her point of view at all. *You'd think she'd be extra nice to me, after I've worked so hard for the honor roll and everything,* Jessica thought with irritation.

"And then I decided to kill Mara Renfrew with arsenic because it's so easy to get hold of," Amanda Howard was saying from the TV screen.

Jessica looked at Elizabeth in disgust. Her sister was hanging on every word.

"But of course, only a car wreck designed to look like an accident would do for Reverend Holiday. . . ."

After another nerve-racking minute, Jessica snapped. With a quick lunge she grabbed the remote and clicked onto her station. Chef Crêpe had just set out all his ingredients.

"All right, and there are the eggs," he was saying. "Later today, after we tour the Loire Valley, our special guest star, Jean Voilan, is going to show us his own special recipe for Oysters Flambé. I'm sure we'll all be looking forward to that."

Jessica squealed happily and scooted back farther on the couch. Jean Voilan was the totally hunky star on her favorite soap, *Days of Turmoil*. She could never have too much Jean Voilan.

"Excuse me!" Elizabeth said angrily, as she grabbed the remote back. She pressed the buttons for her channel. "First come, first served. And my show is definitely more important than this dumb program!"

"It is not," Jessica said, outraged. "How can you say that little old lady is more important than Jean Voilan! Didn't you see him rescue Skyler from that burning building just last week?"

Elizabeth's eyes narrowed. "Earth to Jessica," she said sarcastically. "He's an *actor*. It was a fake burning building on a *soap opera*. And I can't believe you'd rather watch a stupid cooking show than an important *literary* program. Maybe you're not ready for the honor roll after all."

"Oh!" Jessica gasped. That was a low blow. Leaping over Elizabeth, she grabbed the remote again, punched in her channel, and stood right in front of the TV with her arms folded.

"The important thing to remember is to have your

eggs at room temperature," Chef Crêpe was saying.

"You better turn back to my station," Elizabeth said in a warning tone.

A whirring sound came from the TV.

"No way!" Jessica snapped.

"A little cream of tartar will make the whites whip up very fluffy and high, very beautiful," Chef Crêpe said. "Oh, look at that! Like the Swiss Alps!"

"Jessica! I can't believe you! Quit being such a jerk!"

Jessica's jaw tightened; so did her grip on the remote.

On the TV screen, Chef Crêpe demonstrated his whipped egg whites. "You just want to dive into them, eh?" he said.

"Oof!" Jessica was almost knocked off her feet by a huge hurled sofa pillow. "Elizabeth!" she screamed, scrambling out from under the pillow. Instantly, she grabbed another pillow and whacked Elizabeth in the stomach with it. Elizabeth doubled over and rolled on the ground to get out of Jessica's way.

"Oh! I'll get you for that!" Elizabeth screamed, taking cover behind the couch.

"They don't call me the French Einstein for nothing," Chef Crêpe boasted. "Never have I seen egg whites like this."

Quickly, Jessica put the remote in her mouth so both hands would be free. Leaning over, she picked up the pillow Elizabeth had hit her with.

"Kuhm aw out," she said. "Fie lie uh man."

Elizabeth crouched lower behind the couch, her face contorted angrily. "Go jump!" she cried.

"Now we break for the commercial," Chef Crêpe said reluctantly. "When we come back—soufflé city!"

Suddenly Jessica sensed that someone was behind her. She whirled to see Steven, the twins' fourteen-year-old brother, coming into the family room. He looked from one sister to the other: Jessica standing at the ready with a huge sofa cushion, Elizabeth cowering behind the couch. He shook his head, then plucked the remote out of Jessica's mouth with an air of distaste.

"Yuck," he said, wiping it across the back of Jessica's shirt. "Don't tell me—you're on the new electronics diet."

He sauntered over to the couch, flopped on it, and casually flicked to a baseball game.

One pair of outraged blue-green eyes met another pair.

"Steven!" both twins wailed. "We were watching TV!"

"No you weren't," he said in a bored voice. "You were fighting with the sofa cushions." Leaning over, he scooped up one from the floor and tucked it behind his head. On the TV, a guy in a white uniform caught a ball. "All right!" Steven punched the air. "Junior Griffey is king."

Jessica was about to scream at him, but she decided that might not be the best tactic. Instead, she dropped her sofa cushion weapon, smoothed her hair, and came to sit on the arm of the couch. "Steven," she said calmly, "please give me the remote. I was right in the middle of *Lifestyles of the French and Famous*."

"Take a hike," Steven offered, not even looking up.

"*I* was right in the middle of an Amanda Howard

interview," Elizabeth said, still panting from the battle as she came out from behind the couch.

"You're mistaking me for someone who cares," Steven said, his eyes glued to the TV screen.

"Steven!" both twins screeched. Jessica grabbed for the remote, but Steven easily held it out of her reach.

"Look, kids," Steven said. "You have two choices. Either you can get out of my hair and let me watch this game, or you can be pounded into submission. You decide."

Jessica's fingernails dug into the sofa cushion, but she had to admit defeat. She knew her older brother was all too capable of holding her down and giving her noogies on her head until she gave in.

"I'm going," she spat out. She glared at Elizabeth. "This is all your fault," she snarled.

"Uh-uh," Elizabeth snarled back. "You know it's yours, Ms. Honor Roll."

At this Steven actually looked up. "Jessica? On the honor roll?" He gave a short bark of amusement. "Yeah, right. When pigs fly."

If I stay here, I will kill him, Jessica thought furiously. So she turned on her heel, stalked out of the family room, and stomped upstairs, where she banged her bedroom door loudly.

Two

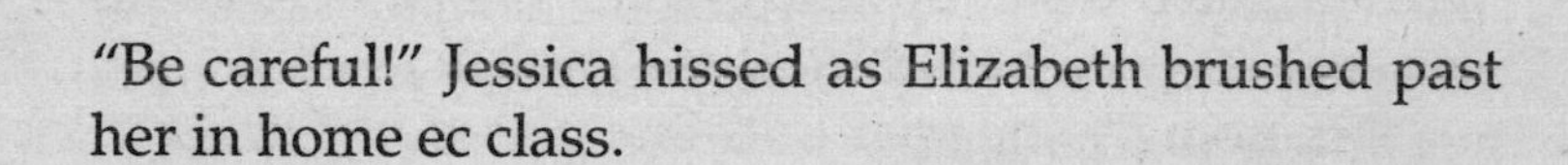

"Be careful!" Jessica hissed as Elizabeth brushed past her in home ec class.

"Go soak your head!" Elizabeth snapped back. "And make it ice water, to bring the swelling down."

Jessica clenched her fists. *I think I prefer the silent treatment,* she thought furiously. Since their fight yesterday afternoon, the twins had hardly spoken a word to each other. Now Jessica pulled her stool as far away from Elizabeth's as possible. Elizabeth carefully pulled her backpack away from Jessica's side, as if it would be contaminated if it touched her sister.

At the next cooking station, Lila waved at Jessica. Lila was also a member of the Unicorns and the Boosters, but more than that, she was the daughter of one of the wealthiest people in Sweet Valley. She and her father lived alone in a huge mansion not far from Jessica's house. She and Jessica had been best friends, and sometimes best enemies, for a long time.

"Oh, my gosh, did you see *Lifestyles of the French and Famous?*" Lila whispered, leaning over toward Jessica. "Jean Voilan is one total babe! When he set those oysters on fire, I thought I would die."

"Gee," Jessica answered with a pained expression, feeling as if she would scream. She *knew* Jean Voilan was totally adorable. Everyone knew that. Except for old blockheaded Elizabeth. "As a matter of fact, I *didn't* get to see it yesterday."

Lila's brown eyes went wide. "You missed Jean Voilan? Why? How?"

"Ask my pigheaded sister," Jessica said. "She insisted on watching some stupid interview instead, and while we were arguing about it, Steven came in and stole the remote." The very memory made Jessica feel angry all over again.

"Well, why didn't you guys just tape one show while you were watching the other? Doesn't your VCR do that?"

A stifled gasp behind her made Jessica turn around. Elizabeth was biting her lip. It made Jessica realize she was doing the same thing. Yes, of course their VCR did that. The twins had often taped one show while watching another. But they had been too angry the day before to think of it, and so neither of them got to watch her show.

"Sheesh, Jessica," Lila continued. "I can't believe you just let Jean Voilan slip through your fingers like that. I mean, when's the next time he'll be on *Lifestyles of the French and Famous?*"

Feeling even angrier, Jessica flipped her blond hair over her shoulder and faced the front of the class. "Be quiet, Lila. I'm trying to pay attention to Mrs. Gerhart."

Lila snickered and scooted her own stool back. At the front of the class, Mrs. Gerhart was getting ready to hand out a photocopied sheet.

"Now, on this sheet you'll find a basic sugar-cookie recipe," the teacher was saying. "You'll split up into your usual cooking teams, and each team is responsible for one batch of cookies. I've put out all sorts of spices, flavorings, and decorations so that you can personalize your cookies. You'll be judged on how well you follow instructions, your technique, your presentation, and the final result. The team with the best cookies at the end of class will get a ten-point extra credit."

Jessica's ears pricked up. Ten points extra credit! That was exactly what she needed to nudge her grade point average onto the honor roll. This was perfect! Her home ec grade hadn't been exactly stellar before now. There had been that strawberry shortcake disaster a while back, though she still thought it hadn't been *all* her fault. And the basic-budgeting workshop had caused her grade to nose-dive. But here was the perfect chance to pull up her grade and make this month's honor roll! And of course, once she was *on* the honor roll, it would be a cinch to *stay* there. A quick image of herself at eighth-grade graduation flitted through her head. "As valedictorian, I have a responsibility to academic excellence. . . ."

Next to her, Elizabeth was grumpily pulling out canisters of flour and sugar and gathering her utensils together.

"Come on, Jess," she said impatiently. "If you think I'm going to do all the work, as usual, you're crazy. Go get the eggs and the butter from the refrigerator." She slapped a set of measuring cups on the counter.

Jessica's nostrils flared. Without deigning to reply, she went to get in line for eggs and butter. *That is so like Elizabeth,* she fumed. *Always trying to boss me around. Taking charge. Running everything. Like I'm too much of an airhead to be responsible for my own work.* When she got up to the front of the line, she realized she had left the recipe back at her workstation. "Just give me whatever you gave everyone else," she snapped at Caroline Pearce, who was helping to hand out the butter and eggs. Then, with her hands full, she made her way back to Elizabeth.

"Let's cut ours in circles and decorate them like basketballs," Todd Wilkins was saying to his partner, Aaron Dallas.

Aaron nodded eagerly. "Cool. We can make stripes out of black licorice."

"I'm going to add special flavoring to ours," Lila was telling Ellen Riteman, another member of the Unicorn Club. "We can base it on a cookie I had in Italy once. They call cookies biscotti over there."

By the time Jessica got back, Elizabeth had already measured out the flour and sugar. Her mouth was set in a grim line, and she didn't look at Jessica.

"Cream the butter and the sugar together," Elizabeth said shortly. "And be sure you measure them correctly. Don't make any stupid mistakes."

That did it. Jessica slammed the butter down on their counter with a squishy thump.

"Nobody died and made you boss," she snarled. "And I for one don't want to listen to you. I'm breaking up this partnership. You can be on a team all by yourself."

"Fine!" Elizabeth said, sifting the flour briskly. A small cloud of fine white powder rose into the air. "Make your own cookies all by yourself. That'll be a laugh. I just hope Mrs. Gerhart doesn't mind your wasting all the ingredients."

"Ha!" Jessica turned away and began to assemble her own ingredients and utensils. The photocopied sheet had a list of everything she would need, and Jessica carefully checked her stuff against Lila's. *This is going to be a snap,* she thought, opening the canister of flour. All she had to do was whip up a batch of sugar cookies, and those ten points would be hers, all hers. Then she would be on the honor roll, and everyone would be so impressed. Even Elizabeth would apologize.

There was only one problem, Jessica realized as she stared at all the ingredients. She didn't know the first thing about making cookies.

Usually, she left all that domestic stuff to Elizabeth. The only cookies she had ever made were the slice-and-bake kind. They had usually come out OK, she remembered.

Sneaking a glance at her twin, Jessica saw that Elizabeth was already stirring flour into some other mixture. Her brow was wrinkled in concentration as she read the next step of the recipe.

Of course! That was what recipes were for, Jessica thought with relief. All she had to do was read it and follow the instructions, step by step. No prob.

Step 1. Cream the sugar and butter together until light and fluffy.

Frowning, Jessica reread her list of ingredients. Cream wasn't listed anywhere. How the heck could she get cream out of butter and sugar?

Jessica looked around. Everyone in class was busily stirring or sifting or already rolling out their cookie dough. They seemed to have solved the cream problem somehow. At the next table, Lila slapped Ellen's hand away.

"Quit eating the raw dough!" Lila scolded. "Leave some to bake, OK?"

"It's just so good," Ellen said meekly.

"Well, you're going to make yourself sick," Lila said.

Jessica decided to start with what she knew. She knew how to sift flour. At least, she had just seen Elizabeth do it.

"Goodness, Jessica," said Mrs. Gerhart, looking over her shoulder. "You'd better hurry. Preparation time is almost over."

A tingle of alarm went down Jessica's spine. She needed these ten points. No other class grade would be as easy to pull up. Feeling panicky, she took a huge mixing bowl and threw the flour in without sifting it. Then she dumped in all the other dry ingredients: baking soda, baking powder, salt . . . salt? That had to be a mistake. She checked the recipe. Yes, salt.

She grabbed a smaller bowl and broke some eggs into it. *The little pieces of shell will probably just dissolve when they're baking,* she figured. Then she took a stick of softened butter and mushed it into the eggs as best she could. It looked pretty disgusting. Deciding to just forget about the cream altogether, Jessica grabbed the canister of sugar. She scooped out a cupful, and hesitated. She hadn't sifted the flour—would it help at all to sift the sugar now?

Maybe I better ask, she thought. Her whole ten points was riding on this.

"Elizabeth," she began in a small voice, turning to her sister.

But at that moment Elizabeth was bending over to pick up a wooden spoon she had dropped. When Jessica turned to face her, Elizabeth suddenly straightened up, bumping into Jessica's cup of sugar, which spilled all over Elizabeth's shirt.

"Jessica! Look what you did!" Elizabeth said, trying to brush the sugar off her shirt. "Thanks a lot!"

"I didn't mean to," Jessica protested. She put down the sugar and tried to help brush the sugar off Elizabeth's shirt, but her hands were sticky and she only made the problem worse, smearing butter and raw egg across Elizabeth's front.

"Stop it—just leave me alone!" Elizabeth snapped.

"OK, class, two more minutes," Mrs. Gerhart announced.

"I was only trying to help!" Jessica snapped back. "I didn't do it on purpose!"

"I guess you're just a klutz, then!" Elizabeth said.

"Who are you calling a klutz, you bossy witch?" Jessica said, waving a wooden spoon threateningly at her. "I don't need to take this from you."

"Jessica!" said Mrs. Gerhart.

Startled, Jessica whirled, and her wooden spoon knocked a bunch of flavorings into her mixing bowl. With dismay Jessica quickly picked out the small bottles and bags and tossed them aside. What a disaster! She might as well kiss the honor roll good-bye. And it was all Elizabeth's fault.

Feeling totally disgruntled, Jessica made one last-ditch effort to salvage her cookies. *When in doubt, accessorize,* she thought. There were some tiny bottles of food coloring on the counter, and Jessica took the red and the blue.

Red and blue make purple, she remembered. Purple was the Unicorn Club's official color, since it was the color of royalty. Sighing, Jessica added several drops of each color to her batter. Purple always looked good. *Couldn't hurt now.* Or could it? The dough was now a strange, unhealthy purple shade. *I guess purple looks good as long as it isn't on a cookie.*

With a pathetic groan, Jessica despondently dropped spoonfuls of dough on her cookie sheet. Maybe if she did an extra book report or two for English. She could write about Jean Voilan's new biography or something.

"Mmm, those look rad, Elizabeth," Todd said, looking over her shoulder. "Totally edible."

Elizabeth smiled up at him. She and Todd had been friends their whole lives, and lately they had been practically boyfriend and girlfriend.

"Thanks," she said, continuing to sprinkle colored sugar carefully on top of the cookies on her cookie sheet. She lowered her voice. "I added a tiny bit of orange flavoring, too. I hope it worked."

"I bet it did. You always have good ideas," Todd said loyally.

"I can't wait to see your basketball cookies," Elizabeth said. Next to her, she heard Jessica give a little moan. Looking up, Elizabeth saw that Jessica was glopping disgusting *purple* batter in lumps onto her cookie sheet. After giving Todd a startled glance, Elizabeth studied Jessica again. Her twin looked miserable. There was flour in her long hair, and bits of butter and dough all up and down her arms. There was even a streak of sugar on her cheek.

Despite her anger at Jessica, Elizabeth couldn't help feeling slightly sorry for her, too. Her lumps of batter were all uneven, and Jessica was trying to smooth them out with a spoon. They were sticky and were peaking up like little purple waves.

Poor Jessica. How does she always manage to do this?

"Heavens, Jessica. What happened?" Mrs. Gerhart asked, coming around to inspect the cookie sheets before they went in the oven.

Elizabeth saw a light of panic in her sister's eyes. "Oh, these aren't mine," Jessica said quickly. "I'm just helping Lila and Ellen with their—"

"You are not!" Ellen said firmly from her table. "We didn't have anything to do with that revolting mess. You're on your own, Jessica Wakefield."

"That's right!" Lila confirmed. "Our biscotti would never come out so disgusting."

"Well, let's just see what happens when they bake," Mrs. Gerhart said doubtfully. She moved on to the next cooking team. "Oh, very nice, Sophia. You and Amy have done a lovely job of decorating your cookies."

Everyone lined up to put their cookie sheets in the four big home ec ovens. When Elizabeth returned to her cooking station, Jessica looked even more miserable than before. Her lower lip was pushed out, and she was slowly gathering all the utensils she'd used.

Poor Jessica, Elizabeth thought again. True, her sister could be incredibly annoying sometimes, but she usually meant well. Some of these bizarre scrapes she got herself into really weren't all her fault. There was just something about her that seemed to attract trouble.

While the cookies baked, the class loaded their dirty bowls and utensils into the large industrial dishwashers. Each team put away their ingredients and wiped down the counters. Then there was nothing to do but wait. Elizabeth decided that when they got home that afternoon, she would try to make up with Jessica. She would offer again to help her with her classes. It was the least she could do.

A few minutes later, the first batches of cookies were ready to come out of the oven.

"All right!" Todd crowed. He and Aaron slapped high fives. On their cookie sheet were row after row of orange basketball cookies. They started removing them and putting them on the cooling rack. Mrs. Gerhart beamed at them and picked up a cookie to taste it.

"Delicious!" she announced. "Excellent work, boys."

Todd and Aaron each eagerly took a couple of cookies themselves.

"Oh, no," Maria Slater moaned. The cookies she

had made with Julie Porter had spread out amazingly over their cookie sheet, forming one incredibly thin, massive cookie.

"Looks like too much sugar, girls," said Mrs. Gerhart. She broke off a little piece and ate it. "It tastes OK, though. Why don't you try cutting it into squares with a knife? After it cools, you'll have tasty square cookies."

"OK," Maria said, looking disappointed.

Mrs. Gerhart came to Lila and Ellen's cookies, which were beautiful—pale in the middle and tan around the edges. "These look lovely, girls." She took a bite. "What's that flavor? Anise? Very experimental, and successful. Good for you."

Grinning, Lila flipped her long brown hair over her shoulder. "These biscotti would be great with cappuccino," she said.

Elizabeth grinned to herself. She knew Lila hated cappuccino.

"These look good," the teacher announced when she came to Caroline Pearce and Randy Mason's cookies. Caroline was the biggest gossip in the whole sixth grade, and Randy was a total science whiz. They made an odd cooking team. Elizabeth could still remember their hollandaise sauce. It had practically been a new life-form.

Mrs. Gerhart took a bite of cookie, then immediately stopped chewing. "Water!" she gasped. "Water!" After she had gulped some water, she turned to Caroline and Randy. "I think you measured the baking soda wrong," she croaked. "You better throw these away."

Randy and Caroline looked crushed.

The teacher continued around the room. Most of the cookies had turned out more or less OK, though there were a few spectacular failures, and a couple of really good batches. Finally, Mrs. Gerhart tasted Elizabeth's.

"Mmm, these are really nice," she said, smiling at Elizabeth. "A nice touch of orange. Good job, as usual, Elizabeth."

Elizabeth smiled back, but she dreaded what was coming next. Jessica's cookies.

Three

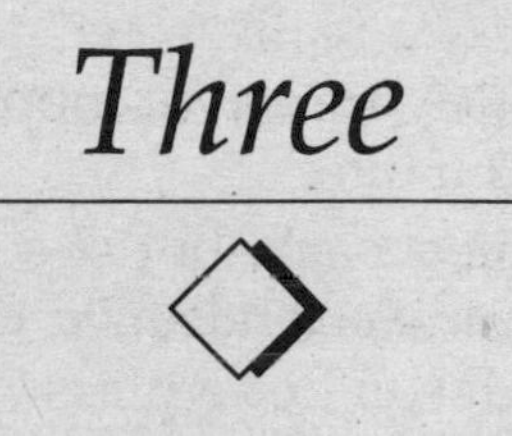

Jessica waited at her cooking station, holding her breath. Her palms were sweaty, and there were still bits of butter and sugar under her fingernails. She didn't care if she never saw another sugar cookie again as long as she lived.

Her own cookies were waiting in little depressed rows on their cooling rack. Their color had lightened a bit to a smooth, even lavender, and Jessica had sprinkled their tops with powdered sugar in an attempt to disguise them. They actually didn't look too bad, which was a good thing, because Jessica was sure they would taste like dog food.

Mrs. Gerhart came and looked at Jessica's cookies. She pulled her glasses down off her nose and looked at them again.

"How . . . unusual," she said, forcing a smile at Jessica. "They're lavender. Almost mauve."

"They're awful. Almost repulsive," Jessica heard

Randy Mason whisper in back of her. *Like he has room to talk,* she thought huffily.

"Yes, ma'am," Jessica said, looking at her shoes. "Maybe I could be judged on presentation alone," she said, having a sudden thought. "You don't have to taste—"

But the home ec teacher scooped up one cookie and gingerly took a bite.

She chewed.

Lila, Sophia, and Aaron leaned forward with anticipation. Randy Mason got a glass of water ready. Jim Sturbridge pulled the trash can closer.

Mrs. Gerhart blinked.

She took another bite.

Maria gasped.

Finally, Mrs. Gerhart swallowed and peered at the lavender cookie in her hand.

"This is absolutely delicious!" she announced.

"Wh-what?" Jessica blurted.

"This is a fabulous cookie, Jessica," Mrs. Gerhart said with a big smile. "The color is unusual, it's true, but the flavor is out of this world. What extra ingredients did you put in?"

This is a fabulous cookie, Jessica, was all that Jessica heard. A fabulous cookie! In front of the whole class, Mrs. Gerhart had called her cookies fabulous! No one else's had been called fabulous. Who cared what the extra ingredients had been?

"It's a secret," Jessica said clearly, giving a big smile.

"Well, they're great," the teacher said. She took Jessica's hand and raised it overhead. "I pronounce you the winner of the best-cookie contest! The ten points of extra credit are yours!"

Jessica beamed happily. What luck! She'd thought these cookies would push the honor roll totally out of her reach, and instead they'd made it possible! She couldn't believe it.

"I don't believe this," Lila grumbled, eyeing Jessica's cookies. She and Jessica were extremely competitive with each other.

"Believe it," Jessica said smugly. "Take a bite. See if they would taste good with cappuccino."

Lila took a big bite and chomped thoughtfully. After a few moments a smile crossed her face. "Hey, this is delici— I mean, this isn't bad." She ate the cookie in a few hungry bites, then reached for a second one.

Todd tentatively took a bite, then nodded in surprise. "This is great," he said. "I wouldn't have guessed that Jessica could cook."

Jessica sat up straighter on her stool. Not only was she going to be on this month's honor roll, but she could also cook! Ellen also took a bite of a cookie, then eagerly finished the whole thing. "Wow. This is practically the best cookie I've ever had," she said. "Way to go, Jessica."

"Thank you, thank you," Jessica said, tossing her hair.

Finally, Jessica and Elizabeth, without looking at each other, took one cookie apiece.

Slowly, Jessica ate her cookie. It *was* delicious. *Jessica Wakefield, you've outdone yourself.*

Over her cookie, she met Elizabeth's eyes.

Elizabeth was still chewing. With sympathy, Jessica remembered the plain old "Nice work, Elizabeth" Elizabeth had gotten for *her* cookies. It was too bad. *Sure, Elizabeth is great and follows instructions and everything,* Jessica mused, *but I guess she doesn't have that extra little spark of creative genius, like some other people. Hope she's not jealous.*

"Congratulations, Jess!" Elizabeth said, disrupting Jessica's thoughts. "You really pulled it off."

Jessica smiled back at her. "Thanks. And I did it all by myself."

"I know," Elizabeth said. "I'm glad."

"Yeah, well." Jessica shrugged. "I think this puts me on the honor roll for this month."

"Great," Elizabeth said, scooping the last of her own cookies off her cookie sheet. "That's what you wanted."

Jessica watched her sister for a few moments. Her life was so great right now—except for her and Elizabeth. She didn't blame Elizabeth for feeling a teensy bit put out by Jessica's success, since *she* was used to being the star student and everything. "Listen," Jessica said grandly, "I'm sorry about earlier."

Her sister looked up and smiled. "Me, too. Let's not fight anymore. I'm really glad your cookies came out OK."

Popping the rest of her cookie into her mouth, Jessica felt a happy feeling spread through her stomach. She'd baked great cookies, made up with Elizabeth, and assured herself a place on the honor roll. Life just didn't get any better than this.

Just as the class was packing up their books for

next period, Mrs. Gerhart came over to Jessica and Elizabeth's cooking station.

"Listen, Jessica," she said in a low voice. "A friend of mine, Antoinette Maresca, has a cooking show on television. She's always looking for new talent. Would you mind if I submitted your cookies to her?"

Jessica's face lit up. "Television?"

"That's right," Mrs. Gerhart confirmed. "If you'd like to think about it—"

"No!" Jessica practically shouted. "I mean, I think it would be a good idea to share my cookies with the public. Which cooking show is it?"

"*Lifestyles of the French and Famous,*" Mrs. Gerhart answered. "Antoinette is the producer. Have you heard of it?"

Jessica's eyes popped open wide, and she met Elizabeth's startled gaze. "Yes!" she cried. "I love that show!"

"Well, if my friend likes your cookies, you just might be on it," Mrs. Gerhart said, smiling.

Jessica gasped. "Oh, my gosh! It would be like a dream come true! I was made to be on that show, right, Elizabeth?"

"I've always said so," Elizabeth agreed, grinning.

That evening when Mr. and Mrs. Wakefield came home from work, Elizabeth and Jessica were doing their homework at the kitchen table.

"I'm used to seeing Elizabeth here," said Mrs. Wakefield, "but I have to say I'm surprised to be seeing double."

Elizabeth grinned at Jessica. "Go on, tell them your news."

"You're seeing double because we're even more alike than usual," Jessica said smugly. "As of next Monday, I'll be on this month's honor roll."

Mr. and Mrs. Wakefield stared at their daughter for a moment.

"Really?" Mrs. Wakefield finally said, a big smile spreading across her face. "That's wonderful, sweetie! When did this happen?"

"This afternoon," Jessica explained. "I got ten points extra credit in home ec class, and it was enough to pull up my grade. So now I have enough points for the next honor roll."

Mr. Wakefield came over and gave Jessica a hug. "That's terrific, honey," he said. "Gee, a daughter on the honor roll. I'm really proud of you."

Elizabeth blinked. *She* was always on the honor roll. Had he forgotten that? Now he had *two* daughters on the honor roll. Jessica was *second*.

"I just can't believe it," Mrs. Wakefield exclaimed, also coming over to hug Jessica. "I've dreamed of this happening. Wait until I tell Grandma and Grandpa. I'm so proud of you! You really must have been working hard."

Jessica beamed and pushed her hair behind her ears. "It hasn't been too hard."

Across the table, Elizabeth was looking down at her textbook. Her parents really seemed happy. And it *was* great—Jessica had never been on the honor roll before. But they sure were making a huge fuss about it. Just last week, Elizabeth had come home with a

100 on her science experiment *and* an A on her English essay, and her parents hadn't gotten nearly so excited.

Well, don't worry about it, she told herself. *What's important is that Jessica made the honor roll—just be happy for her.*

"This calls for a celebration!" Mr. Wakefield said excitedly. "It's not every day Jessica makes the honor roll!"

"You're right!" Mrs. Wakefield agreed. "Jessica, pick whatever restaurant you want. We'll all have dinner out tonight. You deserve it."

Jessica looked surprised and pleased. "Um . . . how about La Maison Jacques?" she asked, naming the fanciest restaurant in Sweet Valley.

"You got it!" Mr. Wakefield said. "I'll call them right now for a reservation."

"I better go change," said Mrs. Wakefield. "Jessica, come with me, and you can tell me all about your great achievement."

"OK," Jessica said cheerfully, following her mother out of the room.

Elizabeth was left alone at the kitchen table. Her algebra book was open in front of her. In a few minutes, she would have to go upstairs and change for dinner at La Maison Jacques. She sighed.

Why am I sighing? I'm thrilled for Jessica. Elizabeth sighed again—she couldn't help it. Since Elizabeth was always on the honor roll, no one made a big deal of it anymore. She'd been on the honor roll since second grade, so she didn't get taken to dinner at La Maison Jacques.

The thing is, I'm on the honor roll because I study a lot and take school seriously. Jessica's on the honor roll because she baked some great cookies by mistake. It seemed unequal somehow.

Then Elizabeth shook her head. *I'm just being petty,* she decided. *Jessica deserves all this attention—it's a big achievement for her,* she thought as she headed upstairs to change.

"Oh, Jessica—I'm glad I caught you," Mrs. Gerhart said the next morning in the hallway. Jessica, Elizabeth, and Lila were on their way to homeroom when the home ec teacher came bustling over. "Yesterday afternoon I took your cookies over to my producer friend, Antoinette Maresca, at the television station."

Jessica felt a quiver of excitement. Was this it? Was this her big break?

"And she loved them!" Mrs. Gerhart announced. "She thinks they're just right for *Lifestyles of the French and Famous.*"

Jessica's mouth dropped open. "Oh, my gosh."

"Oh, my gosh," Elizabeth repeated.

"Oh, my gosh," Lila said also.

"Chef Crêpe would feature your cookies as the guest recipe, and he would ask you a few quick questions on camera. The only catch is that you'd have to make four hundred cookies to be passed out to the studio audience. Do you think you could do that?"

Jessica put her hand to her forehead. She felt as if she were floating on air. This was incredible. This was amazing. Her whole life was finally falling into place—the honor roll, the cookies . . .

"Sure she could!" Lila spoke up. "She could make four hundred cookies—no problem. Right, Jessica?" Lila's elbow jabbed Jessica in the ribs.

"Oh, of course!" Jessica said, nodding hard. "No problem. I could do it in my sleep. Will I really be on *Lifestyles of the French and Famous*?"

Mrs. Gerhart smiled. "Absolutely. My friend said your cookies were the best ones she'd ever tasted. Congratulations, dear. You deserve it." With a final smile, the home ec teacher turned and headed down the hall. In the next second, the homeroom bell rang.

As if in a dream, Jessica floated to her homeroom desk and sat down, a beatific smile on her face. Elizabeth sat next to her.

"Gee, congratulations, Jess," Elizabeth said. "Just one question. How are you—"

A small triangle of folded paper hit her in the shoulder and landed on Jessica's desk. Quickly, Jessica hid it from Mr. Davis, their homeroom teacher, and unfolded it beneath her desk.

EMERGENCY UNICORN MEETING. MY PLACE, 4:00. LILA

Jessica leaned around Elizabeth and nodded at Lila. Wait till the Unicorns heard about this!

"Gosh," Amy Sutton whispered, leaning over toward Elizabeth's desk in science class that morning. "*Lifestyles of the French and Famous*. That's a pretty big show." Amy Sutton was Elizabeth's best friend, and she also worked on the *Sixers*.

Elizabeth nodded. "Yeah, it is."

"Jessica might get discovered on that show. Her cookies might make her famous. Like Mrs. Blossom."

Mrs. Blossom's cookies were sold practically everywhere.

"Um, yeah. I guess that's a possibility," Elizabeth said doubtfully.

"Do you think maybe you'd better interview Jessica for the *Sixers*?" Amy asked. "It's been a while since we had a celebrity interview."

"She's not exactly a celebrity," Elizabeth pointed out quietly, hoping Mr. Hillsboro, their science teacher, didn't notice them whispering.

"Yeah, but she might be," Amy responded. "I mean, with the honor roll thing and all. It could be a great angle: She's a great baker and a top student, too."

Elizabeth sighed again. "I guess you're right. I'll try to interview her tonight."

"Elizabeth? Could you read out your answers to problems one through five, please?" Mr. Hillsboro asked.

Elizabeth read her answers.

"Thank you, Elizabeth," Mr. Hillsboro said. "Those are correct." Instead of moving on to the next problems, he just stood there smiling at her. "You must be very proud of Jessica right now."

"Excuse me?" Elizabeth said. She could feel people turning to look at her.

"She's told me that she'll be on next month's honor roll. You must be so pleased for her."

"Oh, yes. I sure am," Elizabeth said.

"How nice to have two star pupils in the family." Then Mr. Hillsboro turned back to the textbook and called on someone else to read her answers.

"I guess she's becoming a celebrity here at school," Amy whispered. "So you'll do the interview?"

"Yeah, sure," Elizabeth mumbled, not looking up from her book.

"You don't sound very excited about it. Is something wrong?" Amy whispered, looking at Elizabeth.

"Oh, no." Elizabeth shook her head. "Of course I'm excited about it. I'll definitely get the interview tonight." *And I'll just sign it Elizabeth "Chopped Liver" Wakefield.*

Four

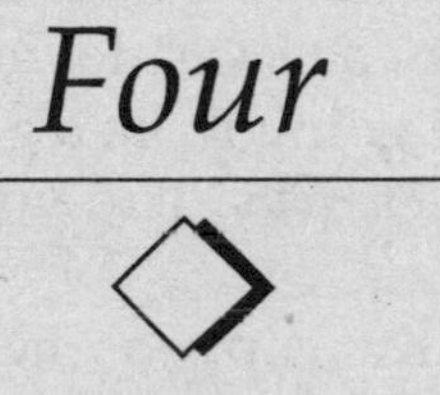

"OK, listen up," Lila said, tapping her milk carton with her fork. It was lunchtime that day, and she and Jessica were sitting with the other Unicorns at the Unicorner, their special table in the cafeteria. "We need to have an emergency meeting today, even though it's a Wednesday. I was thinking four o'clock, my place. Be there or be square."

Tamara, Belinda, and Mandy looked up with interest.

"Is this about Jessica?" Kimberly Haver, a seventh-grade Unicorn, asked.

Lila nodded, and Jessica smiled proudly. She was basking in her sudden fame. Everyone seemed to have heard about her success, and people had been coming up to her all morning.

"Hey," Janet Howell said, "I'm the Unicorn president. I should get to call the meetings." Janet was in eighth grade, and was one of the most important—and bossy—girls in school.

Lila rolled her eyes. "Oh, sorry, Janet. OK, then, do it."

Janet cleared her throat. "I call an emergency Unicorn meeting at Lila's house, today at four."

"Fine," Lila said. "Now, I was thinking—"

"Jessica!" exclaimed Grace Oliver, another sixth-grade Unicorn, as she sat down at the table. "I just heard that you're going to be a guest chef on *Lifestyles of the French and Famous*! Are you going to take over for Chef Crêpe?"

Jessica casually sipped her apple juice and shrugged mysteriously. *Let them all wonder.*

Caroline Pearce rushed over to the table. "Hey, Jessica. Someone told me you were opening your own cookie store at the mall. Is that true?"

Jessica smiled kindly. "Wait and see."

Her eyes widening, Caroline turned and ran off.

"Wakefield," Bruce Patman said as he sauntered up to the Unicorner. "What's this I hear about some famous cookies?"

"What about it?" Jessica asked, beaming sweetly. Bruce was a seventh-grader and as obnoxious as he was cute—which was very. Half the girls at Sweet Valley Middle School thought he was totally adorable, and the other half hated his guts. Jessica went back and forth about it.

"Well, the whole idea of you cooking is a total joke," Bruce went on. "I mean, I heard about how surprised you were when you found out you could use avocados for something besides a facial mask. You couldn't make cookies if your life depended on it." He brushed his thick brown hair off his forehead and looked down his nose at her.

"No, Bruce," Jessica said, still smiling sweetly. "I couldn't make cookies if *your* life depended on it. But when *my* life depended on it, I could, and I did. And they were *très* fabuloso, which is why I'm going to be on *Lifestyles of the French and Famous*." She smirked at him. "And by the way, I've always known there were many uses for an avocado."

Frowning, Bruce looked around the table at all the other Unicorns. "I guess the rest of you birdbrains are going along for the ride," he said finally.

Janet crossed her arms in a huff. "For your information, Bruce—"

"Well, you see, Bruce," Lila cut in, putting a restraining hand on Janet's arm, "we wanted the Unicorns to have a signature cookie—like a designer cookie. We're thinking of calling them 'Unicookies.' Like all Unicorn endeavors, it's a smashing success." She settled back in her chair, a smug expression on her face.

Bruce shook his head. "Unicookies? I won't even *touch* that one."

Jessica watched Bruce walk away, feeling slightly dizzy with confusion. *Unicookies? Signature cookie?* What did the Unicorns have to do with her success?

"Hang on a second, Lila," Jessica began, but she was interrupted by the lunch bell.

"Well, Jess, I'll see you this afternoon at the meeting," Lila said, hurriedly picking up her tray. "Have a nice day!"

After English class that afternoon, Elizabeth wanted to talk to Mr. Bowman.

"I can't believe the news about Jessica's cookies," Cammi Adams said, coming up to Elizabeth after English class. "You must be so excited."

Elizabeth was standing by Mr. Bowman's desk, waiting to talk to him about her interview with Jessica for the *Sixers*. Besides being her English teacher, he was also the faculty adviser for the sixth-grade newspaper.

She mangaged to smile at Cammi. "Oh, yeah, we're all real excited," she said as Cammi left the room.

Mr. Bowman finished erasing the blackboard and came back to his desk. "So, Elizabeth, I hear we have another Wakefield on the honor roll."

Once again, Elizabeth made herself smile. "Yeah. We're really proud of her." *And I* am. *I just wish I could hear about something else once in a while.*

"So with Jessica on this month's honor roll, I guess you'll probably be trying for the principal's list," Mr. Bowman continued cheerfully.

"What do you mean?" Elizabeth asked.

"You know, the principal's list. It's a step up from the honor roll. You have to have A-pluses in all your subjects to get on it, but if anyone could do it, you could."

"Really?" Elizabeth asked, blushing. Then she shook her head. "Thanks, Mr. Bowman, but the fact that Jessica's on the honor roll doesn't mean I should do even better—I mean, I don't want to compete with her or anything."

"You wouldn't necessarily be competing against her," Mr. Bowman said. "But it's reasonable to want to develop your own natural talent, the way she's developing hers. Anyway, think about it. I'd be glad to help you."

"Thanks, Mr. Bowman," Elizabeth said, suddenly forgetting what she'd been waiting to ask him. "It's something to think about. I'll see you later."

"The principal's list?" Amy asked. She had been waiting for Elizabeth outside English class so they could walk to science together.

Elizabeth had quickly filled her in on what Mr. Bowman had said.

"Oh, I've heard about that," Amy said. "It's for real brains. But I'm sure you could get on it if you tried. You're probably not that far away from it now."

"Do you think it would be, well, bad for me to try it?" Elizabeth asked hesitantly.

Amy stared at her. "Bad? How could it possibly be bad to try to do well?"

"You know. Because of Jessica. Do you think people would think that I was just trying to show her up or something?"

"I don't think so," Amy said seriously. "You've always been a great student. It seems natural that you would try for the principal's list. And I think it's not really like you're trying to show Jessica up—more like you're trying to preserve your own individuality."

"Really?" Elizabeth still felt doubtful.

"Yeah. I mean, how would Jessica feel if you suddenly wanted to do all the same things that she does? She might try doing something different, just to feel more *Jessica*, if you know what I mean. Being on the principal's list is a way for you to feel more *Elizabeth*. I think you should go for it, if you want to."

Elizabeth smiled at Amy gratefully. "Thanks, Amy. That makes me feel much better about it."

"What are friends for?" Amy asked with a grin.

"Pass the chips, please," Tamara Chase asked Jessica.

Jessica sat up in her lounge chair and tossed the bag of chips at Tamara.

The Unicorns were gathered around Lila's pool on Wednesday afternoon. It was a warm, sunny day, and Jessica wished she had brought her swimsuit. She hiked her skirt a little bit to tan her legs.

"Careful, Jessica," Belinda Layton said. "You don't want to get too much sun before you go on TV."

Jessica smiled at her and moved her legs back into the shade.

Janet Howell tapped her diet soda can against the patio table. "I might as well call this meeting to order, since we obviously all just want to talk about Jessica. Where's Lila?"

Lila bustled up, carrying a tray of more drinks and a plate of cookies. "Right here. I'm ready for the meeting." She passed out the drinks and cookies. "Of course, these cookies don't compare to Jessica's." She gave Jessica a big smile.

OK, something's up, Jessica thought, smiling back at Lila. She bit into a cookie and was pleased to discover that Lila was right—they weren't as good as hers.

"OK, then," Janet continued. "Let's talk about Unicookies."

"Unicookies?" Jessica asked suspiciously, bristling at that word for the second time that day.

"Let's face it, Jessica," Lila said, sitting on a lounge chair. "These cookies of yours could be the best thing that ever happened to the Unicorns."

"But—" Jessica began.

"Look, Jessica," Janet interrupted. "We're the Unicorns. We're a *club*. We stick together, no matter what, right?"

"Oh, like when Ellen and Lila refused to help me out during home ec class?" Jessica said.

"Jessica." Lila crossed her legs and smoothed her skirt in her lap. "We all know that the cookies are *your* famous recipe. *You* came up with it. It was *your* brilliant baking instincts that created them."

"That's right." Jessica sniffed.

"But here's the thing," Lila said earnestly. "Think of what these cookies could mean for the Unicorns. I meant what I said to Bruce—they could be our signature cookie. These cookies could make all of us famous, the whole Unicorn Club. Unicookies—they're even the official color of the Unicorns. Sure, they're your recipe. No one could forget that. But in a way, if they're Unicookies, you would be twice as famous."

"Oh, yeah?" Jessica asked skeptically. It seemed to her that she should simply have all the fame herself.

"Look at it this way," Ellen Riteman broke in. "Either the cookies are the brainstorm of one sixth-grade girl—in which case maybe they're just a fluke—*or* they could be yet another huge success in a long line of huge successes of the famous Unicorn Club. We're already the most important, most powerful girls at Sweet Valley Middle School. These cookies could make us invincible. And if the Unicorn Club is invincible, and you're a member of the Unicorn Club . . . *you'd* be twice as important. Don't you see?"

"Hmm," Jessica mumbled thoughtfully. When Ellen put it that way, it did sort of make sense. A little sense, anyway.

"There are some other considerations," Janet said importantly. "For example, your own standing within the Unicorn Club. It would sure go up. And as you know, I'm going to be at Sweet Valley High next year. The Unicorns will need a new president."

Jessica drew in her breath. President of the Unicorn Club! It was something she had only dreamed about.

"Not only that, but you need to make four hundred cookies for the studio audience," Lila pointed out. "You could make them all yourself, of course . . . or you could have all of us helping you."

Jessica had to admit, she had a point. After all, four hundred cookies was quite a lot of cookies. And even if the whole Unicorn Club was involved, Jessica could still be the star.

"OK," she said finally with a big smile. "On two conditions: One, I get interviewed first by Chef Crêpe, because it's my recipe. Two, we call them Unicookies, but I sign my name to every box."

A frown flickered across Janet's face. She and Lila met eyes across the patio.

"Because, otherwise," Jessica continued, "I just don't know if—"

"Deal," Janet said briskly.

"Great! Unicookies they are!" Jessica said.

"Three cheers for Jessica," Kimberly said, holding up her lemonade.

"Hip, hip, hooray!" the Unicorns cried.

Jessica sat back in her lounge chair, smiling with pleasure. She could definitely get used to this.

"Well," said Mandy Miller after the cheering had died down, "now that that's settled, and we're all in it together, you can let us in on the secret ingredients. What did you put in your cookies to make them so delicious?"

The smile on Jessica's face faded a little. "The secret ingredients?"

"Extra vanilla?" Grace Oliver asked, her dark eyes shining.

"Chopped pecans?" Mary Wallace suggested.

"White chocolate?" Mandy put in.

Jessica cleared her throat. *The secret ingredients. Right. The secret ingredients were . . .* She remembered that some stuff had fallen into her batter—but what had it been?

"Fruit extract?" Kimberly pressed, starting to look a little exasperated.

Jessica noticed that her heart was beating extra fast. All the Unicorns seemed to be staring at her.

"Jessica," Janet said, folding her arms, "we don't have all day, you know."

Jessica took a deep breath. *Relax,* she commanded herself. There was really nothing to worry about. She'd be able to come up with the secret ingredients, no problem. After all, the whole Unicorn Club was helping her, and the TV show wasn't until the following Tuesday. There was plenty of time to figure out the recipe and make the cookies.

"Come over to my house tomorrow afternoon," Jessica said confidently. "I'll reveal the famous Wakefield secret then."

Five

"Ah! Sugar cookies!" Jessica said to herself as she flipped through the dessert section of one of her mother's cookbooks. She was in her bedroom after dinner, and spread out on the bed all around her were various cookbooks she'd taken from the kitchen. Quickly, Jessica turned to the right page. She knew it—this was going to be a snap. But when she read the recipe, it sounded just like the recipe Mrs. Gerhart had passed out. Nothing unusual. Nothing that clued Jessica in on what she had done to make her cookies so good.

The next book had a list of sugar-cookie variations. Some of them called for ginger or cinnamon, or candy decorations, or for cutting them out in fancy shapes. Jessica hadn't decorated hers, besides sprinkling them with powdered sugar, and she hadn't cut them out. She had no idea whether she had used spices or not, or what they had been. Vaguely, she remembered some sort of pale liquid running through the batter. What could it have been?

Might as well get this over with, Elizabeth thought, grabbing her notebook and her favorite pen. Usually she loved working on stories for the *Sixers,* but interviewing her sister seemed a little pointless. After all, she already knew Jessica practically as well as she knew herself.

She tapped twice on Jessica's closed door, then poked her head in. Jessica was wiggling around on her bed, arranging her covers.

"Jess? Do you have a minute? The *Sixers* would like an exclusive interview for our next issue," Elizabeth told her. "You know, about the honor roll and the cookies and all."

Jessica beamed at her. "Sure! I mean, I *was* just going over some math problems, but I think I can fit an interview into my schedule."

"Good." Elizabeth came in and cleared some laundry off Jessica's desk chair. As usual, Jessica's room looked like the "after" pictures of a major hurricane. Books, magazines, and tapes were strewn on the floor; clothes, both clean and dirty, were piled everywhere; and Jessica's desk was a jumble of hair ornaments, nail polish, and a couple of used dishes.

Elizabeth grinned, looking around. "Maybe we should get the staff photographer to take a few shots of your room. You know, the environment of a girl genius."

"Hardy har har." Jessica made a face. "Why should I waste my time on housework when I'm so busy studying, getting on TV, et cetera, et cetera? Now. Don't you have some questions to ask?"

"Oh, yeah, let's just jump right in." Elizabeth referred to the notes she had jotted down that afternoon. "OK. In the last week you've gone from being a regular student to an honor roll television celebrity. How are you handling the transition?"

Jessica looked very serious and flipped her long blond hair over her shoulder. "I'm glad you asked that question, Elizabeth. I think others could learn from my example. Basically, I'm trying to keep a strong sense of self. Like, it's important to keep the same values and all. Sure, I might be an overnight sensation. I might have tons of people falling all over me. And next week I could be a major television star. But what's important is . . ."

Blah, blah, blah, Elizabeth thought, trying to write down everything Jessica was saying. *Good thing this isn't going right to her head or anything.*

". . . the key word, I think, is inspiration," Jessica continued enthusiastically, looking up at her ceiling. "A lot of people don't realize that baking is more than just making something people are going to want to scarf down. It's a real art form. Inspiration is really important. We artist/geniuses have to get in touch with our innermost feelings, constantly searching for that spark of life, that lightning bolt of inspiration that pushes the average cookie into being a transcendent cookie, for example. I remember when I was younger . . ."

Golly, Jess. We're talking about cookies here, not the cure for cancer, Elizabeth thought with surprise. *And it's not like they're going to take your cookies and display them in the Sweet Valley Fine Art Museum.* Elizabeth's hand was starting to cramp up from writing so fast. She should have brought her tape recorder. Except then she'd have to listen to all this again.

She held up one hand, stemming Jessica's flow of words.

"Yes? Is there something else you'd like to know?" Jessica asked.

Elizabeth consulted her notes again. "Jessica—I remember when you knocked the flavorings into your bowl by accident. You and I were arguing, and things got out of hand. Doesn't it seem that it wasn't so much inspiration as just, well, clumsiness, pure and simple?"

Jessica stared at Elizabeth for a moment. Then she looked at her fingernails. "I'm not so sure about that, Elizabeth," she said. "You see, one thing most major artists have in common is that we have to open ourselves to the possibility of finding inspiration in anything, anywhere, at any time." She paused, gazing around her room thoughtfully. "You know, like, in the falling of a leaf from a tree. The gentle drip of rain in the spring. A cloud passing overhead."

"Some flavoring dropping into your bowl," Elizabeth offered.

"Exactly." Jessica smiled. "The point isn't that it was an accident—the point is what I *made* of the accident. See?"

"Ah, yeah, I guess so."

After a few more questions, Elizabeth stood up, flipping her notepad shut. "OK, Jessica, that should do it." *That should more than do it, frankly.* "This will be in next week's issue."

"Front page?" Jessica looked hopeful.

"Well, if it's a slow news week," Elizabeth said, unable to hold back a grin.

"OK. Thanks, Elizabeth. I won't forget about you when I have my own TV show."

"Thanks, Jess. You're the best," Elizabeth said quickly, shutting Jessica's door behind her.

Suddenly, Elizabeth remembered that she hadn't asked Jessica about the four hundred cookies due next week. Without knocking, she opened Jessica's door a crack. Jessica was engrossed in a book on her bed and didn't hear Elizabeth.

Frowning, Elizabeth quietly shut the door again, her question forgotten. What was Jessica doing with the *Julia Crumpet Baking Book*? Elizabeth had the suspicion that Jessica's fame might already be starting to unravel.

"OK, guys, before we get started, I wanted to go over some of the basics," Jessica told the Unicorns in a professional tone. They were standing in the Wakefield kitchen, where Jessica had set up several different cookie-baking work stations. She was pleased with her newfound organizational abilities, even if she still didn't have a clue how to bake her famous cookies.

"How about this basic: What's the secret ingredient?" Kimberly said, and the other Unicorns laughed.

"All in good time," Jessica promised. "I've been thinking about our presentation for the TV show on Tuesday."

"Our presentation?" asked Grace. "Aren't we just going to have platters of cookies?"

Jessica gave Grace a sympathetic glance. "No, Grace. This is about the whole Unicookies *concept*. Presentation is everything. Now, first thing I was thinking is that we should all wear official Unicorn outfits."

"We don't have Unicorn outfits," Tamara pointed out. "Only Booster costumes."

Jessica sighed. "Look, guys, just try to keep up with me on this, OK? I *know* we don't have Unicorn outfits. But we should try to dress at least a little alike, to show that we're a group, a club. I was thinking we should all wear purple and white, like the cookies. Anything purple and white. That way, when we're on camera or walking around the studio, we make an impact."

"That's a really good idea," Janet Howell said. She leaned over to Jessica. "President material," she whispered.

Lila grimaced a little.

Jessica smiled smugly, feeling a glow of happiness. "Next, I was thinking about the cookies themselves. Any middle-school kids could just show up with cookies on a platter." She glanced at Grace, who blushed.

"But we're the Unicorns," Jessica continued. "We're special, unique. Everything we do is the best, right?"

"Right!" everyone chorused.

"So I think we should go with white bakery boxes. Ellen, maybe you could make a few calls and locate some, price them. Inside each box we should have either white or purple doilies, whichever's easier to get. Belinda, I'm putting you in charge of doilies." Jessica consulted her list.

"Janet, is that OK with you?" Belinda asked.

"Um, yeah, that sounds OK." Janet shrugged helplessly.

"OK, now, each box will be sealed with a purple sticker. And then I'm going to take a purple marker and sign each box *Jessica Wakefield's Unicookies,* in big letters." Jessica sat back, feeling incredibly proud of her plan.

Kimberly frowned a little and crossed her arms. "Jessica, you can't just give everyone orders. Can she, Janet?"

"Yeah," Mary said before Janet could answer. "I thought we were all going to do equal stuff. But we're doing the grunt work, and you're getting all the glory."

"Excuse me," Jessica said, feeling impatient. "Who came up with this recipe?"

"You," Kimberly admitted. "But—"

"Who did Mrs. Gerhart get onto *Lifestyles of the French and Famous*?" Jessica pressed.

"You," Mary said reluctantly.

"Case closed," Jessica said. She consulted her clipboard. "Unless someone has something else to add." She looked out at the Unicorns pointedly. No one said anything.

"Look, I guess it all sounds OK," Janet said finally. "But, Jessica, and this is a big but, first we have to have these fabulous cookies to go in the fancy boxes with the doilies and the stickers and the big writing. Now, it's already Thursday. We have to have four hundred cookies by Tuesday. I say we get started baking right away. We can make three batches a day and freeze them. By Tuesday we should have all the cookies we need."

"Good plan," Lila said. "I agree with Janet—we should get started."

"OK, OK," Jessica said, standing up. "Here's the recipe." She waved the photocopied sheet around. "Divide up into teams of three, and we'll each make a batch."

"One thing, Jessica," Lila said, folding her arms across her chest.

"Yes?"

"What about the secret ingredient?" Lila asked.

Jessica paused. The stupid secret ingredient. Well, there was nothing else she could do. She would just have to wing it. Fortunately, since she was so smart, it should be easy.

"OK, Lila, cool your jets," Jessica said casually. "I'll tell you what: Each team makes a batch of cookies, and then I'll come around and put in the secret ingredients." She glanced at the row of flavorings and spices she had lined up on the counter.

The Unicorns grumbled quietly as they worked, but soon three batches of dough were ready.

Janet slapped Ellen's hand away from their batch. "Leave it alone," she cried. "You've already eaten half of it."

"I'm sorry," Ellen said in a small voice. "Raw cookie dough is my weakness."

"Well, go sit down or something," Janet said impatiently. "At this rate we'll have to make a whole batch just for you, and another batch for the studio audience."

Looking sheepish, Ellen went to sit at the Wakefields' kitchen table.

"Come on, Jessica," Tamara Chase said. "Let's get these cookies done. I have to go home in half an hour."

"Coming, coming," Jessica said. She had thought long and hard about the secret ingredients. That day in home ec class was blurry, but she vaguely remembered liquids of different colors spilling across her dough, as well as a pale, powdery substance. After examining her mother's flavorings and spices, she thought she had the answer.

She lined up the three batches of dough on the counter, then carefully added pineapple flavoring and licorice essence to the first batch. "Ta-daaa!" she said, trying to sound confident.

"Interesting," Mandy said approvingly.

"What a daring combination," Janet said, awe in her voice.

"Let's go ahead and bake these," Jessica said. "Then we can experiment with exactly the right amount of flavoring." At the last minute she remembered the powdery stuff, so she dumped some ginger in. After the food coloring was added, Jessica took a spoon and dropped the cookies in lumps onto a couple of cookie sheets.

Lila popped them in the oven and set the timer with a flourish. "Mmm," she said. "I can't wait for them to come out. Those cookies really were the best cookies I've had in a long time."

"*Naturellement*," Jessica said in her best French

accent. "Come on. We can watch *Lifestyles* while we wait for the cookies to bake."

"Look," Lila said when they were all settled in the family room. "The guest today is Jean-Marc Espalier. Isn't he that new French rock star?"

"All I know is he's gorgeous," Janet cooed.

"Not as gorgeous as Jean Voilan, though." Lila sighed. "Wouldn't it be great if Jean Voilan came back to guest-star again, on the same day as us?"

"It would be total heaven," Jessica agreed. "But I don't see how it could happen. He was on just last Monday. *Days of Turmoil* must keep him pretty busy."

Then the timer went off and the Unicorns raced to the kitchen.

"What's that smell?" Kimberly asked, wrinkling her nose.

"Did we burn them?" Belinda wondered.

"No," Jessica said, pulling the cookie sheets out of the oven. "They look fine." *But different.* She put the cookie sheets on the counter to cool, and the Unicorns gathered around anxiously.

"Hmm. These cookies aren't the pretty, smooth lavender of the batch you made at school," Janet said.

"Yeah. They're more of a sick mustardy color, with strong purple overtones," Ellen said critically.

"They smell weird," Tamara said bluntly.

"I, uh, must have messed up with the food coloring," Jessica said nervously, peeling up one cookie with a spatula. "But I'm sure they'll taste OK."

With eight beady pairs of Unicorn eyes on her, Jessica took a small bite. *Oh, no!* It tasted incredibly awful. It took all of Jessica's self-control not to spit the cookie immediately into the sink.

"Yum, I can't wait," Janet said. "Let's all just have a little taste—you know, to celebrate our first batch."

"But—" Jessica began, but it was no use. The Unicorns were enthusiastically biting into cookies. Then eight Unicorns made gagging noises and leaned over the kitchen sink to spit them out.

"Oh, double gross," Jessica complained, turning on the disposal. "You could have swallowed them."

"No," Tamara gasped, taking a drink of her juice. "I couldn't. I really couldn't. That was the most disgusting cookie I've ever had in my life."

"Don't even call it a cookie," Lila begged, fanning her mouth with her hand. "You'll depress all the other cookies in the world. Cookies that are worthy of the name."

"One thing is clear," Janet said, after she had rinsed her mouth several times. "Those were the wrong secret ingredients."

Jessica bit her lip miserably as eight pairs of Unicorn eyes homed in on her accusingly.

Six

"I must have misread the labels," Jessica said meekly. "Maybe I used the wrong amount. Let me try again."

Janet crossed her arms and wordlessly pointed at the two remaining batches of cookie dough.

With a smothered sigh, Jessica peered at all her mother's spices and flavorings again. The answer had to be here. It was right in front of her eyes. *Think, Jessica, think.*

When Elizabeth opened her front door that afternoon, the first thing she heard was heated yelling coming from the kitchen.

"I keep telling you—" Jessica was saying.

"Look, Jessica," Janet cried, "if you don't want to tell us the secret ingredient, fine. But quit wasting our time!"

"Yeah," Kimberly agreed loudly. "I would take

these cookies home to my dog, but I love my dog too much. They stink!"

Elizabeth quickly headed down the hall. When she pushed open the door to the kitchen, she gasped. All she could see was a huge mess and a bunch of screaming Unicorns. There wasn't a clean surface or an unused bowl or utensil in sight. The floor was tracked with floury footprints, the refrigerator had smeared handprints, the oven door was hanging open and dripping batter. Jessica was in the middle, waving her arms and shouting back at Janet.

"Hey!" Elizabeth clapped her hands loudly, and the Unicorns jumped.

"Hey, Elizabeth," Jessica said sulkily.

"What happened here?" Elizabeth demanded. She put her heavy backpack and her library books down on a kitchen chair. "This place looks like Hurricane Cookie hit it. What have you guys been doing?"

"You mean besides listening to Jessica spout off about cookies, which is a total joke?" Janet sneered. "We've been facing disaster, that's what!"

Tamara Chase angrily grabbed her backpack and her purse. "I have to get home—I'm late already. All I can say is, you better get it together, Jessica." She stomped out of the kitchen and slammed the front door behind her.

"Look, let's all cool down," Elizabeth said soothingly. "Everyone just relax for a minute." She took out the carton of juice from the fridge and refilled everyone's glass. She had never seen so many sullen Unicorns in her life, and that was saying something.

"OK, now," Elizabeth said. "Mandy, why don't you tell me what happened."

All the Unicorns started shouting again, and Elizabeth held up her hand. "I asked Mandy," she said firmly.

"Well," Mandy began, shooting an angry glance at Jessica, "in short, we tried to make our Unicookies. But Jessica won't tell us the secret ingredients."

"Yeah," Ellen jumped in. "We've made three different batches of cookies, and they're all Gag City. She wants to keep the secret for herself."

"I *thought* we were all in this together," Lila said accusingly. "But she wants to cut the Unicorns out."

"No, that's not it," Jessica began.

"Oh? Then what *is* it, Jessica?" Janet demanded.

"Yeah. How come you've wasted our whole afternoon?" Belinda asked with a frown.

Elizabeth banged on the counter for attention.

"Please!" she said. "Let Jessica talk. Jess, what's going on?"

"Well, it's . . ." Jessica looked down at her shoes, which were spattered with dough, butter, and flour.

Janet tapped her sneaker against the Wakefields' sticky floor. "Yes?"

"I . . . don't actually remember the secret ingredients," Jessica whispered.

"You what?" Janet shrieked.

Elizabeth stepped in between her sister and Janet. She knew how hard it was to admit to being wrong—especially for Jessica. "Look, look," she said quickly. "OK, so she forgot. These things happen. It's not anyone's fault, really. But you have four days before

Tuesday. I'm sure if you all work together, you'll pull it off. Aren't you always saying that the Unicorns can do anything?"

"We just need to experiment some more," Jessica said, shooting Elizabeth a grateful glance.

"That's right. How hard could it be, especially for the Unicorns?" Elizabeth asked coaxingly. "You guys are at your best when you're under a little pressure." She felt kind of phony, sucking up to the Unisnobs, but it was for a good cause.

Kimberly looked doubtful, but the others began nodding their heads.

"I guess that's true," Janet said, brushing her hair off her face.

"We always manage to get it together in the end," Belinda said, nodding. "The Unicorns always come out on top."

"Yeah," said Mandy. "We're the best. If we can't do it, no one can."

"That's right, guys," Jessica said. "I know we can blow the cookie market wide open. It's just a matter of fine-tuning the recipe."

There, I've done my part, Elizabeth said, taking an apple out of the basket and picking up her backpack and books. *The rest is up to you, Jess.* "I'll let you guys get started," she said, heading out of the kitchen. "But I'm sure it'll be another big Unicorn success." She left before they could see the smile on her face.

"OK, look," Janet said after Elizabeth had left. "Elizabeth made some good points. We *are* supposed to be in this together. And the Unicorns *can* do just about anything. That's why we're Unicorns. That's why most girls *aren't* Unicorns. But, Jessica, you would have saved us a lot of time if you had just told us you had forgotten the secret ingredients."

Jessica looked embarrassed. "I figured it would just come back to me once we started baking," she explained. "I wasn't trying to keep them secret, honest."

"What do we do now?" Mandy asked.

"We just have to keep experimenting," Kimberly grumbled. "We'll try a little of this and a little of that. Sooner or later we'll get it right."

"Yeah," Mary said enthusiastically. "How hard could it be? After all, we *are* the Unicorns, like Elizabeth said."

"OK, then, are we all agreed?" Janet asked. "Do we all want to keep working with Jessica on the Unicookies, and try to be on *Lifestyles of the French and Famous*?"

"Yeah," Ellen said. "Count me in."

"Me, too," Lila said.

The others voted to stick together also.

"Let's get started right away," Belinda said, pushing up her sleeves. "Tuesday will be here before we know it."

"There's just one more problem," Jessica said in a small voice.

"What now?" Kimberly demanded.

"We're all out of butter and eggs," Jessica said, pointing to the empty cartons on the counter.

"Oh." Janet frowned. "Well, it's getting late anyway. Why don't we wrap it up for today, and tomorrow afternoon we'll start fresh."

"We can meet at my house tomorrow," Lila offered. "I'll ask Mrs. Purvis to get us plenty of everything we need."

"Thank you, Lila," Janet said graciously, patting her hair into place. "Your kitchen is nice and big—a real chef's kitchen. I'm sure we'll be successful tomorrow."

"OK, then," Lila said, gathering up her things. "Someone call Tamara and tell her. I'll see you all at school tomorrow. 'Bye, Jess."

"Good grief!" Mrs. Wakefield exclaimed, coming into the kitchen a few minutes later. "What in the world happened here?"

Jessica looked up in surprise, then followed her mother's gaze around the room. "Ulp," she said. Somehow the state of the kitchen hadn't seemed so important a minute ago, when the Unicorns were all angry with her, but now she saw what Elizabeth had meant about Hurricane Cookie. Every countertop was covered with dirty bowls, wooden spoons, mixing tools, measuring cups, and used cookie sheets. The sink was full of disgusting discarded cookies, piled high and soggy with water.

Jessica cleared her throat. "Um, me and the Unicorns—"

"Looks like the Unicorns are gone," Mrs. Wakefield said severely, cutting her off. "So you'll have to clean this all up by yourself."

"Me?" Jessica squeaked. "By myself? I only made one-ninth of the mess."

"You," Mrs. Wakefield confirmed. "And be quick

about it. Your dad and Steven will be home soon, and we have to get some kind of dinner together."

"But—but—" Jessica sputtered.

"Honestly, Jessica," her mother said, heading upstairs. "I would have thought that someone on the honor roll would have a little more sense."

That did it. Jessica's eyes narrowed, and she flung back her long blond hair. With a yank she pulled open the dishwasher door and started loading it.

Seven

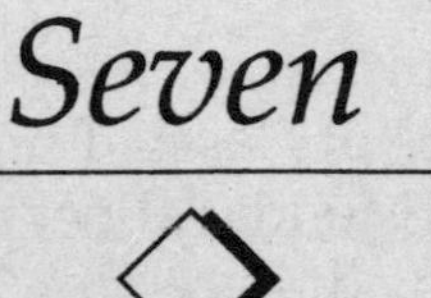

#7. Which amendment to the Constitution gave American women the right to vote? In what year was this amendment ratified?

Elizabeth chewed on her pencil. She knew this. Ah.

The nineteenth amendment, ratified in 1920, gave women the right to vote.

Elizabeth was glad she had brushed up on her history notes last night. It wasn't often that there was a pop quiz on a Friday, but she had prepared for it, just in case.

She answered each question carefully. It was important that she get 100 on this quiz. Her usual 95s and 98s weren't good enough anymore. Everything had to be 100 from now on, until she made the principal's list. She didn't have too much further to go.

The second hand swept around the clock. After

Elizabeth had answered the last essay question, she quickly reviewed her test. *Looks good,* she thought with a smile. She had done her best. All she had to do was keep this up for a couple of weeks, and the principal's list was hers.

"That pop quiz was a total bummer," Amy groaned at the end of class. "I hadn't even gone over the material since Monday. I bet my grade just sunk a couple points. How did you do?"

Elizabeth shrugged casually as she gathered up her books. "I think I did OK. I had just reread some of my notes last night, after I finished working on my extra-credit book report for English."

"You're lucky," Amy sighed. "I bet you aced it. Well, at any rate, I guess I'm ready for the algebra test. At least I studied for that."

Elizabeth stopped dead in her tracks. She stared at Amy as other students wove around them on the way to class.

"What do you mean?" Elizabeth asked.

Amy smothered a yawn. "You know. The algebra test on chapters nine and ten. Ms. Wyler told us about it last week." She suddenly paused in alarm and looked at Elizabeth. "You *did* study for it, didn't you?"

Elizabeth slowly leaned her head against the wall. What a nightmare. "I can't believe we have an algebra test today," she moaned.

Amy gazed back at Elizabeth. "Oh, Elizabeth," she said sympathetically.

* * *

"What are you doing this afternoon?" Elizabeth asked as she and Jessica walked home from school on Friday. "Want to go to Casey's with me?" Casey's was their favorite ice cream place at the mall. *If anything could make me forget about that crummy algebra test, ice cream could.* She figured she passed it with a lousy B—and a B just wasn't good enough if she wanted to make the principal's list.

"I wish I could," Jessica said, "but I have to change my clothes and head to Lila's. We're going to be working on the Unicookies again."

"Oh. Have you tried extra vanilla?"

"We've tried lots of things," Jessica groaned as they turned down Calico Drive. "To tell you the truth, I wouldn't care if I never saw another cookie again in my life." She hung her head, and her long blond hair fell forward. "Oh, Elizabeth, how do these things happen to me? All I wanted was to make the honor roll. Then I got a chance to be on *Lifestyles of the French and Famous*. Is that so terrible? Why must I go through this torture?"

A glimmer of a smile passed over Elizabeth's face. *Jessica really should be an actress,* she thought. *She can make anything sound dramatic.* "Don't worry, Jess," Elizabeth said to soothe her. "I'm sure the Unicorns will help you figure out the recipe. And if worse comes to worst, and you can't duplicate them exactly, just dye regular sugar cookies purple and show up anyway."

"Elizabeth!" Jessica looked aghast. "I couldn't do that! Chef Crêpe is expecting the best cookies in the world! I would be totally humiliated."

"You're going to be totally humiliated anyway, if

you have *no* cookies," Elizabeth pointed out.

Jessica moaned again.

"Look, Jessica, I'm sure you'll get it together," Elizabeth said reassuringly as they came to their own house. "I bet—"

Jessica lifted her head. "What am I doing?" she demanded, a new glint in her eyes. "I'm letting negative vibes ruin my whole future."

Elizabeth unlocked their front door. "Well, I understand why—"

"After all, I'm Jessica Wakefield," Jessica said, interrupting. "I'm a Unicorn. I'm on the honor roll, starting Monday. I baked the most fabulous cookies the world has ever seen. What am I moaning about?"

Together the twins trooped upstairs.

"It's good to think positively, Jessica," Elizabeth said, marveling at her sister's ability to completely turn her emotions around.

"That's what I'm going to do from now on," Jessica vowed as she went into her room and dropped her backpack on the floor. It fell with a gentle thump onto a pile of fashion magazines. Jessica took off her school clothes and flung them across her desk, then started pawing through her piles of laundry. "I don't need sympathy from anyone. I'm sure that today is the day," she said, her voice muffled as she pulled on her T-shirt. "We'll figure out the recipe, and make four hundred totally intense cookies, and this time next week, I'll be a star."

"Well, that's great," Elizabeth said, leaning against the door frame.

"*Lifestyles of the French and Famous* is only the beginning," Jessica continued, gathering her hair back into a ponytail. "Years from now, I'll look back on this whole thing and laugh."

"I sure hope so," Elizabeth said mildly.

Suddenly, Jessica went up to Elizabeth and gave her a big hug. "Thanks, Lizzie," she said happily. "I feel much better now. You always know the right thing to say. Now, I'm off to Lila's. Tell Mom where I am, OK?"

"Sure thing," Elizabeth agreed.

Jessica pounded down the stairs, humming a little tune under her breath. She slammed the front door cheerfully behind her.

"Ow," Steven said, coming out of his room with his hands over his ears. "What was that?"

"That," Elizabeth said, "was the future cookie queen of Sweet Valley."

"Right. And you're the next president of the United States," Steven replied. "Ow!" he said again as Elizabeth punched him on the way to her room.

"OK, Unicorns!" Janet Howell clapped her hands. "Let's come to order!"

"Yeah, let's get going," Lila agreed. "Mrs. Purvis will be back around dinnertime, so we want to have everything done by then. She left us all the stuff we'll need."

The Unicorns were gathered in Lila's large, sunny kitchen. At one end of the kitchen were sliding glass doors that led to the patio and the pool.

"That water looks great," Mary muttered longingly.

"Yeah," Mandy agreed.

Janet cleared her throat. "Now, the first order of business is, of course, the Unicookies. To refresh everyone's memory, Jessica doesn't have a clue what's in them."

Jessica, sitting on a bar stool at the kitchen island, grimaced. She really didn't think anyone's memory needed refreshing.

"We know that they're mostly a basic sugar-cookie recipe with a few secret ingredients," Janet said, gesturing to the piles of flour, sugar, butter, and eggs waiting on one counter. "We know the ingredients were present during home ec class, so it's not anything totally bizarre that only Jessica could know about. And finally, we know that we have to duplicate Jessica's first batch of cookies if we want to be on *Lifestyles of the French and Famous*. Any questions?"

"Yeah," Kimberly Haver said. "What if we can't duplicate them?"

Janet glared at her briefly. "Any questions that aren't negative?" she asked, looking out at her fellow Unicorns. No one said anything. "OK, then, split into teams of three, and let's start mixing!"

Jessica, Lila, and Ellen worked together at one section of a counter. By now they all practically knew the recipe by heart, and it didn't take long to get a batch of dough together.

Then Janet came around, armed with several flavorings and spices. "Now, Jessica says it was a combination of several things, as well as she can remember—which isn't very." Janet glanced briefly at Jessica, who bit her lip. "But let's just try several different things." After examining her bottles, Janet sprinkled in some cinnamon, some orange flavoring, and some mint flavoring.

To Kimberly, Mandy, and Mary's batch, she added vanilla, root beer flavoring, and some nutmeg.

The batch she had worked on with Tamara and Belinda was doctored up with allspice, almond flavoring, and lemon.

Then Mary and Belinda put the cookie sheets into the two wall ovens and set the timer.

"I feel good about this," Jessica said firmly. "I know one of these batches will be the one. Then all we have to do is make a whole lot of them. On Monday night, we can put them into our boxes and seal them up, ready for the TV show."

Mandy smiled at her encouragingly. "Sounds like a plan."

Five minutes later, they took the cookies out of the ovens. Each batch was a nice even lavender color.

"At least we got the food coloring down," Lila muttered. Then she stared pointedly at Jessica. "I think Jessica should be the official taster."

"Yeah, absolutely," Ellen said. "I still have a bad taste in my mouth from yesterday's cookies."

"Yeah, yeah," Jessica said dismissively as she pried one cookie from each batch with a spatula. She considered saying something about how everyone would eat their words, but she decided against it. Everyone's eyes were on her as she took a big bite of the first cookie. She chewed.

"Well?" Mandy Miller demanded.

"It's not bad," Jessica said, swallowing. "Really not too bad. Kind of orangey and minty. And cinnamony. But it isn't a Unicookie."

"OK, try another one," Mary Wallace urged her.

The second cookie was harder to get down. The root beer flavoring was definitely a mistake. Jessica didn't bother saying anything—she just swallowed hard, took a sip of water, and made the thumbs-down sign. Everyone groaned.

Finally she took a bite of the third cookie. Janet and Tamara moved closer, staring at her intently.

"Well, these aren't bad," Jessica said, trying not to let disappointment into her voice. *Keep positive.* "You might even say they're good."

"Are they Unicookies?" Lila asked eagerly.

"Well, no," Jessica admitted.

Tamara and Janet groaned, and Ellen banged her hand on the counter, raising a small cloud of flour.

"What are we going to do?" Belinda wailed. "This is never going to work! We made three batches yesterday and three batches today, and all we've done is make ourselves sick! It's hopeless. We'll never get on TV." Putting her head down on the counter, she closed her eyes and sniffled.

"Wait a minute," Lila said, her brown eyes starting to gleam. "I have an idea—I got it from a TV show last night."

"What is it?" Tamara said glumly.

"Look, our whole problem is that Jessica can't remember what the secret ingredients are, right?" Lila asked.

"Duh," Kimberly said sarcastically.

"So all we need to do is *make* Jessica remember," Lila finished excitedly.

Jessica looked at her in alarm. *Make* her remember?

What was Lila planning? Beating her? Torture? Tickling her to death?

"Hypnotism," Lila announced. She stood with her arms on her hips and nodded her head decisively.

"Hypnotism?" Jessica exclaimed.

"Yes," Lila said, coming closer. "I saw a whole program about it last night on TV. This woman had witnessed a crime but couldn't remember it—she had blocked it out. So they hypnotized her, and then she could identify the suspects. Her subconscious remembered!"

Janet leaned forward in interest. "So if we hypnotize Jessica, maybe she'll see the secret ingredients again!"

"Exactly." Lila looked incredibly pleased with herself.

Jessica looked at Lila skeptically. "I don't know, you guys. I—"

"It's a great idea," Mandy said. "How can we hypnotize her?"

"It looked easy," Lila said. "Let's go into the family room, where we can lower the blinds. And I need a candle, and something shiny, on a chain."

Five minutes later Jessica was sitting warily on a leather ottoman in Lila's family room. The Unicorns had drawn the blinds, and the room was in semidarkness.

"Where's Lila?" Jessica asked nervously.

"She's getting all the stuff," Janet answered.

"What stuff?" Jessica asked nervously, picking at a thread on her shorts.

Janet came up behind Jessica and massaged her

shoulders briskly. "Just try to relax, Jessica. This won't hurt a bit."

"Hurt?" Jessica repeated. She hadn't considered the possibility of pain.

"And think of how fabulous it'll be when you remember the ingredients!" Janet continued. "All tomorrow and Sunday and Monday we can just make cookies, no problem, and then on Tuesday we'll all be totally famous."

Lila burst into the family room and sat on her father's BarcaLounger, facing Jessica. She lit a long white candle and handed it to Tamara.

"OK, Tamara. Sit next to me and hold the candle where Jessica can see it," Lila commanded. "How do you feel, Jessica?"

"Um, why don't we just rethink this?" Jessica answered.

Lila waved her hand impatiently. "Just relax. This isn't going to kill you. OK. The first thing you have to do is empty your mind of any thoughts at all. Just let yourself float freely."

Jessica tried not to think about anything, but it was impossible. Across from her, Lila was fiddling with something shiny. Finally she held it up—it was a silver pendant on a silver chain. She let it dangle in front of Jessica's eyes, then started swinging it gently back and forth.

Jessica's hand shot out and grabbed it. "What the heck is this thing?" she demanded, examining it. "It's a . . . a tooth! A silver tooth. Oh, gross me out!" She dropped it again.

Lila frowned at her. "It's not a real tooth," she explained impatiently. "It's my Tuffy the Tooth good-patient charm. My dentist gave it to me when I didn't have any cavities for a year."

"Couldn't you use something else?" Janet asked. "That *is* kind of gross."

"It's not a real tooth!" Lila cried. "It's just a charm. What do you want me to use—my real ruby necklace? Get over yourself." She turned back to Jessica, still frowning. "OK, now, relax and concentrate. Just clear your mind, focus on the charm, and have the candle be sort of in the background."

Sighing, Jessica tried to watch the silver tooth charm as it swung slowly back and forth, its silver roots pointing down. The candle was glowing behind Lila's head, and Lila was speaking softly in front of her.

"You're getting sleepy," Lila was saying. "Your eyelids are getting heavier. Soon you'll close your eyes, but you'll still be awake. Then I'll lead you back several days into the past . . . back to last Tuesday, when you made cookies in home ec. . . ."

Today's Friday, Jessica realized happily. She had almost forgotten. So tomorrow she didn't have to get up early, and tonight she didn't have to do homework. She could wait until Sunday to do it.

"OK, now, close your eyes," Lila intoned, still swinging Tuffy the Tooth.

Jessica closed her eyes.

"You're in home ec," Lila droned on. "You're sharing a table with Elizabeth. You guys are arguing. You start to mix your own batch of sugar cookies. . . ."

Maybe tonight Elizabeth and I could go to a movie at the mall, Jessica thought. *That new comedy just opened. That would be fun. We could get Mom to drive us. Maybe we could even get a slice of pizza first at the food court.*

"OK, Jessica," Lila said. "Your cookie dough is all finished. But something happened: something spilled into your batter. You quickly take something out. Tell me what bottles you picked out of the batter, after they spilled. Jessica? Jessica?"

If we go to the early movie, maybe afterward we would have time to go to Valley Fashions. I could use a new cropped sweater.

"Gee, she's really asleep," Mandy murmured. "Lila, what have you done?"

"Jessica?" Lila raised her voice a little. "Jessica!"

At the sound of her name, Jessica opened her eyes. Lila was peering at her anxiously, and the other Unicorns were all hovering around.

"What?" she said.

"Are you still out?" Lila whispered, looking concerned.

"Out where?" Jessica frowned. "Out of what? What are you talking about?"

The Unicorns groaned, and Lila looked frustrated.

"Weren't you hypnotized just now?" Lila asked. "Weren't you just in the home ec room, looking at all the flavorings?"

"No," Jessica said. "Was I supposed to be?"

All the Unicorns groaned again.

"This isn't working," Janet announced. "It was a good idea, Lila, but I guess Jessica just isn't susceptible. Nice try, though."

"It's getting late," Mary said. "I better be getting home."

"Yeah," Kimberly agreed. "Tamara, you want to walk home with me?"

Tamara sat behind Lila, still holding the candle perfectly still.

"Tamara?" Kimberly said. "Tamara?"

"What, Mrs. Gerhart?" Tamara answered slowly. "Can't I use sprinkles on top of my cookies? Elizabeth did."

Jessica's eyes went wide, and she looked at Lila in alarm. Tamara was staring off into space beyond the candle's flame.

"Oh, my gosh," Lila whispered. "It worked on Tamara!"

"Well, snap her out of it," Janet cried. "It's time to go home."

Lila stood frozen, staring at Tamara.

"Lila, come on. Get her to wake up," Kimberly urged.

"Um, well—" Lila stammered.

"Lila!" Belinda exclaimed.

Lila looked up sheepishly. "I don't know how to wake her up. I changed the channel before the hypnotism show was over."

"Well, try something!" Janet practically screeched. "We can't just drop her off at her house like this! Her parents will freak."

Lila snapped her fingers in front of Tamara's face a couple times. "Come on, Tamara," she said. "Wake up. Let's go. Home ec is over now."

But Tamara sat quietly, holding her candle.

Eight

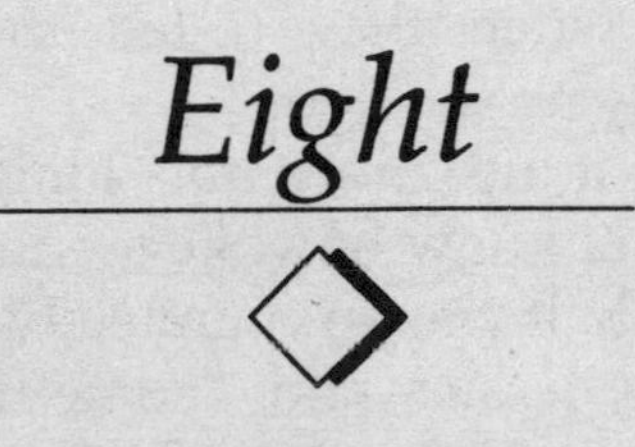

"I'm sorry, Lila," Jessica said over the phone. "I'm not doing it on purpose."

Lila lay down on her bed and put her feet up against the wall. "Are you sure you're trying as hard as you can? I just don't know how much more of this I can take."

Lila and her father had just come back from dinner, and Lila was in her room trying to recover from the horrible day the Unicorns had had at Janet Howell's house. It had been a totally wasted Saturday, as far as she was concerned.

"Hey, you think I enjoyed what we went through today?" Jessica asked defensively. "I feel like if I even smell another sugar cookie, I'm just going to barf."

"I know what you mean. And having Joe and Steven there sure didn't help."

Joe Howell was Janet's older brother, and he happened to be best friends with Steven Wakefield.

Naturally, when the Unicorns were totally in the middle of cookie production, the boys had descended on the kitchen and tormented everyone.

"They're such jerks," Jessica said angrily. "I mean, today's cookies were failures. I admit that. But it wasn't funny when they tasted them and rolled around in agony on the floor."

"They kept it up much too long," Lila agreed. "And I still don't know how Steven made foam come out of his mouth. It was so completely repulsive."

"He's gross," Jessica said. "Sometimes it's hard to believe we're related. Anyway. To change the subject, how's Mrs. Purvis today?"

Lila sighed and tapped her feet against her Johnny Buck poster. "She's better. She'll get over it. It's not like *she* has to pay to unclog the kitchen disposal. All she has to do is wait for the repairman."

"How long are you banned from using the kitchen?"

"Two more weeks," Lila told her gloomily. "It's like this cookie disaster is affecting every aspect of my life. I still can't believe that you just can't remember the ingredients."

"Oh, give me a break, Lila!" Jessica protested. "I can't be expected to memorize every little thing in the world, you know."

"Every little—" Lila began, then cut herself off. This argument was starting to wear her out. "Anyway, this whole kitchen mess is really Tamara's fault. I thought we'd never get her out of that trance. If it hadn't taken so long to snap her out of it, we could have cleaned the kitchen before Mrs. Purvis got home. Then none of this would have happened."

"Yeah," Jessica said, sounding weary. "At least Tamara did finally wake up. It was pretty creepy. I thought she was going to end up going to high school like that."

Lila giggled. "Maybe that wouldn't have been so bad. She was so agreeable when she was in her trance."

"We'll have to remember the technique for later," Jessica said with a giggle. "Like, 'Tamara, lend me some money so I can get the latest Johnny Buck CD.' 'Oh, OK, Jessica.'" Jessica giggled again, then she sighed. "Look, I'm going to go take a shower. I just found some butter in my hair. I'll see you at Belinda's tomorrow, right?"

"Uh-huh," Lila said unenthusiastically. "Ten o'clock. I can't believe we have to do this again."

"Me, too. But look, if we get it right, we'll all be on *Lifestyles of the French and Famous*," Jessica pointed out. "Then it'll all be worth it."

"Yeah. OK, see you tomorrow."

After she had hung up with Jessica, Lila lay around on her bed for a little longer. What a horrible day she'd had. Yesterday had been horrible, too. Her whole life had been horrible lately, and it was all because of these stupid cookies.

And no matter how hopeful she and the other Unicorns acted, the dreadful truth was becoming more and more obvious: They would bomb on *Lifestyles of the French and Famous*. Tuesday would come, and they would show up at the studio with empty hands. Or even worse, with four hundred of the most disgusting lavender cookies that anyone had ever seen. Jessica was Lila's best friend, and Lila didn't want to make her feel worse than she already felt, but really, it *was* all sort of Jessica's fault. If they didn't get it together about the cookies, next Tuesday the Unicorns would be totally disgraced and humiliated on national TV.

Lila chewed on her thumbnail. She pictured herself, in a cute purple-and-white outfit, passing out white boxes of cookies to the studio audience. She pictured people taking a cookie. She pictured someone taking a bite of cookie, and then staring at Lila in horror and dismay. Would a total stranger really spit out a mouthful of cookie like that, right in front of Lila and everyone else? Would the studio audience drop to the ground and writhe on the floor in agony after tasting the cookies, as Joe and Steven had? Would the Unicorns stand there in humiliated shock, holding their horrible death cookies as all of America stared at them?

Lila groaned and rolled off her bed. She couldn't let it happen, she just couldn't! She had to protect herself, the Unicorns, and even Jessica. But what could she do? Bake four hundred cookies all by herself? Yeah, right. Lila stood in front of her mirror and picked up her hairbrush. She started brushing her long, brown hair with firm, even strokes. Brushing her hair always helped her think. More than once, in the middle of some awful test at school, she had wished she could brush her hair. It would definitely help pull her grades up if she could.

OK, think, Lila, think, she commanded herself. *You're a Fowler. What would a Fowler do? What would Dad do in this case?*

Lila paused. Maybe she couldn't bake four hundred cookies, but she could always pay someone else to bake them. Now, would Mrs. Purvis do it? Lila wrinkled her nose. Not after the ugly scene in the kitchen the day before.

Lila thought harder. There had to be a million bakers in Sweet Valley. Surely one of them could come up with four hundred purple cookies if the price was right.

Lila sat down at her vanity table and tapped her brush against her chin. But what if someone found out? What if the baker talked? The Unicorns would be exposed as total frauds.

What she needed, Lila mused, was an out-of-town source. A disinterested party. Some cookie supplier who would never know about the TV show, who would never know about the Unicorns. After Lila had thought hard for another minute, her brown eyes started to gleam. "That's it!" she whispered. "That's the answer."

A minute later, she had padded downstairs to the library. Then she began to rummage through her dad's collection of mail-order catalogues.

"OK," she murmured. "Here we go. Gourmet Foods from Switzerland. This ought to do it." Lila riffled the pages until she got to the cookie section. Yes. They had sugar cookies, all kinds. With one finger marking the correct page, Lila reached for the phone.

* * *

"I . . . hate . . . cookies," Ellen Riteman moaned from where she was lying on Belinda Layton's family room floor. Her eyes were shut, and her face was pale.

"Don't even say that word," Mandy whimpered, not taking the cool rag off her forehead.

It was Sunday afternoon. The air was thick with the mingled, cloying scents of sugar, eggs, butter, and vanilla. From the kitchen, the slightly pungent smell of baked cookies wafted through the door.

"I'll never eat another hmm-hmm again as long as I live," Janet murmured from the couch. One arm was draped across her eyes. The other trailed limply along the floor.

"What are we going to do?" Mary wondered, close to tears. "It's Sunday—the show is two days away. Either we have to blow off going, or show up with some wretched Frankenstein cookies that'll get us kicked out of the studio."

"You said that word!" Mandy cried, holding her stomach.

"Look, people," Jessica broke in, trying to sound calm. "Today didn't go as well as we thought it would. OK. Now, all we have to do—"

"Didn't go so well!" Lila broke in, weakly raising her head from the carpet. "It was a total disaster! Let's face it. We're ruined."

"We are not!" Jessica said impatiently. "We still have tonight and tomorrow."

"Oh, big whoop," Tamara said sarcastically. "Thirty-six hours to save our lives from unending humiliation and failure. Every single kid in school is going to be glued to their TV set on Tuesday waiting to see us fail. We'll never live it down. It's probably the end of the Unicorn Club."

"Look, I have an idea," Jessica began desperately.

"Great," Kimberly said. "That's all we need, another one of your ideas."

Jessica folded her arms and glared from one Unicorn to another. "As I recall," she said coldly, "I didn't *ask* you guys to butt your heads into my cookie business. As I recall, you all *begged* me to let you in on the whole TV show thing. It's no skin off my nose if you guys want to ditch now. I'll solve the problem myself, go on TV by myself, and get all the fame and glory by *myself*. Now, do you want to hear my idea or not?"

Slowly, Mandy and Mary raised their heads from the floor. Ellen and Janet wearily met each other's eyes.

"OK. Tell us your idea, Jessica," Janet finally said.

Jessica felt a tiny flare of triumph. She was proud of herself for trying to motivate everyone again. The old Jessica would have just given up by now. The new, honor-roll Jessica was still coming up with solutions, still keeping positive. It was the mark of a leader.

"OK, listen," Jessica said. "This is what I came up with. Tomorrow's Monday. I say we call Mrs. Gerhart tonight, and ask her to meet us at the home ec room tomorrow morning early, before school. I bet in the exact same place, with the exact same mixing bowls and ovens and all, we'll be able to come up with a fabulous cookie right away. It's probably all I need to jog my memory."

"Hmm," Janet said thoughtfully. "That's actually not a bad idea."

"Yeah," Ellen said. "We should have thought of that earlier."

"OK," Mandy agreed, removing her cool rag. "Let's do it. Jessica, you call Mrs. Gerhart. The rest of us will meet you there at seven o'clock in the morning. If Mrs. Gerhart says no, you can call us tonight and let us know."

"Good plan," Janet said. "Let's drag ourselves home now and get rested up for tomorrow. Belinda, what are you going to do with all of today's cookies?"

Belinda sat up and brushed her hair out of her eyes. "I thought I'd put them on Mom's compost pile," she said.

OK, Elizabeth thought, reviewing her assignment book. *Algebra, check. English, check. Social studies, check.* All her weekend homework was complete, and she could face tomorrow morning knowing that she was completely prepared. In fact, she realized, looking at the clock, she still had an hour before bedtime tonight. She could start making preliminary notes for her history project. It was due in two weeks.

Sighing, Elizabeth assembled the library books she would need for the project. Good thing she had chosen her topic early.

A slight tap on her door made her look up. Her mother came in with a glass of juice, which she placed on Elizabeth's desk.

"Thought you might need some refreshment," she said, sitting on Elizabeth's bed.

"Thanks, Mom." Elizabeth took a big swig of juice.

"It's not like you to leave your homework till Sunday night," Mrs. Wakefield said. "I could have sworn you did most of it yesterday."

"I did," Elizabeth confirmed. "Right now I'm just going over everything, and starting a couple of extra-credit projects."

"Extra credit?" Mrs. Wakefield repeated. "Is that why you've been holed up inside for the last two days? Besides that movie you went to with Jessica, you haven't done anything fun this weekend. Are your grades slipping a little?"

Elizabeth shook her head. "No, they're fine. But I thought I would try to bring them up anyway."

Mrs. Wakefield looked thoughtful. "How much higher can they go? You've always made terrific grades."

"Not straight A-pluses," Elizabeth said.

"Goodness, Elizabeth," said Mrs. Wakefield. "Why would you put yourself through this? What happens if you make straight A-pluses in everything? You're already on the honor roll every month."

Oh, so you remembered, Elizabeth thought, a little surprised. She tapped her foot against her desk leg. "I get on the principal's list," she explained quietly.

"And that's higher than the honor roll?"

Elizabeth nodded, not meeting her mother's eyes.

"I see." Mrs. Wakefield stood up, then came and kissed Elizabeth on her forehead. "That would be wonderful, honey, and we would be so proud of you. But of course, we're always proud of you, no matter what you do. So if you want to achieve this goal, make sure you're doing it for yourself."

"OK, Mom," Elizabeth said. Her mother left and closed the door behind her. *I am doing this for myself, aren't I?*

Elizabeth opened her first library book, then decided she should probably take a few quick notes as she read. She opened her loose-leaf binder, her pen poised.

Then she stared. Inside her binder was her extra-credit book report for English—the one she was supposed to turn in last Friday.

Groaning, Elizabeth dropped her head into her hands. She'd probably been so upset about the algebra test that she had forgotten about the book report. Now it was too late to turn it in—all that work had been for nothing.

At this rate, I'll never get on the principal's list, Elizabeth thought morosely. It seemed as if the harder she tried to pull up her grades, the more she sabotaged her schoolwork. It was almost as if the principal's list just wasn't meant to be.

Nine

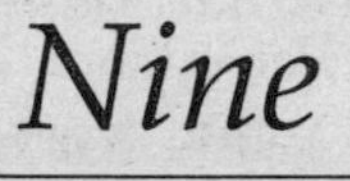

"Good morning, girls," Mrs. Gerhart said, as she unlocked the home ec room door at seven o'clock Monday morning.

"Good morning," Jessica said. The other Unicorns grunted sleepily and slowly shuffled inside.

"Thanks for letting us use this room," Jessica continued, heading to the ingredients cupboard and taking out the things they would need. "Four hundred cookies is a lot of cookies, and we needed this big kitchen." *Well, it's not exactly a lie,* Jessica thought. They *did* need to make four hundred cookies. The fact that they didn't have the slightest idea how to make them was beside the point. They didn't need to worry Mrs. Gerhart with the details.

The teacher settled down at her desk with a cup of coffee and the newspaper.

"OK, now, listen up," Jessica whispered to the other members of the Unicorn Club, who were all looking at her sleepily. "This is our last chance. I know we can do it. Let's split up into our teams, and I'll put all the flavorings out on the counter. I just know it'll come to me when I see them. Is everyone ready?"

"Ready as I'll ever be," Kimberly grumbled, rubbing the sleep out of her eyes.

"This has been so much work," Ellen said wearily, as she measured flour for sifting. "I feel sick when I think about making this batch of batter."

"Me, too," Tamara agreed, sullenly cutting up sticks of butter. "I can't stand the smell of butter anymore."

Jessica sighed in exasperation. "Look," she said impatiently. "Am I sick of cookies? Yes. Am I frustrated by all our failures? Yes. But am I complaining? No. And you know why?" She began to pace in front of the group, looking from one Unicorn to the next. "Because I'm keeping my eyes on the goal, that's why." She looked off into the distance. "Being on my favorite TV show, becoming a star, making the Unicorns a household name. You guys have to look beyond today's pain of making cookies—look ahead to our fame and fortune." She peered once more at the Unicorns. "Understood?"

"Yeah, OK," Ellen said, turning on the electric mixer.

"Fine, fine," Mary grumbled, cutting up some sticks of butter.

Five minutes later, their first experimental batch of cookie dough was ready. Jessica peered at the line of flavorings on the counter. She squinted, trying to cast her mind back to that fateful day almost a week ago. What had been on the counter? What had she knocked into her bowl? She put her head in her hands. There were a million cookie ingredients dancing around in her mind, and they were giving her a headache.

"I can't do it!" she exclaimed, turning her back on the dough. "I can't even think straight. Someone else add the flavorings, OK?"

"OK," Mandy said. "Just go sit down or something before you explode."

Jessica sank into a chair as the flavorings were added.

"You can look now," Ellen said.

Janet mixed the flavorings in well.

Lila added the purple food coloring.

Mandy dropped the batter by spoonfuls onto fresh cookie sheets.

Tamara put the cookies in one of the big ovens.

Belinda set the timer for eight minutes.

Then there was nothing to do but wait. The Unicorns sprawled around the cooking stations, getting ingredients ready for the next batch of dough. They didn't speak. They didn't look at one another. They simply went through the motions like robots.

Just then a messenger came to the door and spoke to Mrs. Gerhart. The teacher stood up and faced the Unicorns.

"Girls, there's a phone call for me at the office. I'll be back in just a few minutes. In the meantime, I expect you to practice excellent kitchen safety habits."

"OK, Mrs. Gerhart," Jessica said, and Mrs. Gerhart left the room.

Janet put her head down on her hands on top of a work surface. "I can't bear to smell them cooking," she moaned. "I don't think I'll ever, ever eat another cookie again. Last night at dinner my brother had a couple of oatmeal cookies, and I almost gagged."

"Oh, stop exaggerating," Jessica said impatiently. "We're all sick of cookies. Quit whining about it."

Janet looked up, her eyes narrowed. "I'm *not* exaggerating. I really did almost gag."

"Yeah, yeah," Jessica said in a bored tone. She picked up her clipboard. "Look, I've calmed down a little now. Just tell me what's in this batch, so I can check it against the log." After the first batch of cookies, they had been keeping precise records of exactly what flavoring combinations they had tried.

"Um, orange flavoring," Mandy said, thinking back. "Or was it lemon? Something citrus."

"I put in some chocolate syrup," Mary added.

"I think I put in some extra sugar," Belinda said.

Jessica stared at them. "You think? You *think*? Didn't you pay attention? Didn't anyone measure anything exactly?"

"Chill out, Jessica," Belinda said huffily. "It's hardly even dawn yet, and we're all working on top of one another. It's hard to keep track of stuff."

Jessica felt as if she were going to explode.

"Belinda! What's the point of doing this if we're not going to keep track? I mean, isn't that the point?" Jessica slammed her palm against her forehead and stomped around the room.

"Jessica, get a grip," Janet commanded irritably. "We're all doing the best we can."

Jessica was about to yell a retort when the oven timer sounded. She and the Unicorns gathered around the oven eagerly. Janet put on a mitt and pulled out the cookie sheet.

Hardly waiting for the cookies to cool, Jessica scooped one up with a spatula and bit into it.

"Well?" Kimberly asked impatiently.

Jessica chewed, her face showing her disappointment. With a great effort, she swallowed the bite of cookie. "It's awful," she said softly.

"Oh, good grief!" Mandy cried, banging her wooden spoon down on the counter. "I can't take this anymore! Let's face it, it's not going to happen."

"Don't say that!" Jessica shouted. "If you all weren't such a bunch of wimps, we would have done it by now!"

"What?" Ellen screeched, staring at Jessica in disbelief. "How can you say that? We've worked just as hard as you!"

"Shut up!" Janet yelled, whacking her metal spatula against the counter. "Everyone just shut up!"

But it was far too late for that.

"It's all your fault!" Belinda screamed at Jessica.

"You're an idiot!" Jessica yelled back.

"You're all totally hopeless!" Mandy shouted above everyone.

In desperation, Janet suddenly smacked Mandy on the behind with the spatula, trying to get her to be quiet. Mandy, enraged, took a big handful of raw batter and smeared it on Belinda's shirt. Shrieking with anger, Belinda slammed Lila over the head with a cookie sheet. Lila wobbled for a second, but recovered almost instantly and walloped Jessica on the shoulder with a wooden spoon.

Completely falling to pieces, Jessica picked up a raw egg and hummed it as hard as she could at Lila. But Lila saw it coming and ducked, and it sailed over her head like a round white missile . . .

. . . until it reached Mrs. Gerhart and splattered against her forehead.

The Unicorns froze.

Jessica felt an icy finger of shock trail along the back of her neck and down her spine. She was so horrified, she couldn't even gasp. She had just slammed a teacher with a raw egg. There was no way to salvage this situation.

Dimly, Jessica was aware of the other Unicorns turning to gaze at her in dismay. This was a new low for the Unicorns, a lowly low so low they might never recover. The lowest.

"*What* is going on here?" Mrs. Gerhart thundered, grabbing a roll of paper towels. She took off her glasses and began wiping her face. Then she stalked to the sink, washed her glasses, and wet more paper towels. In another minute, most of the egg was gone, except for a few specks in her gray hair, which Jessica didn't think she should mention right now.

Janet recovered first.

"We're really sorry, Mrs. Gerhart," she began humbly. "We just . . . lost it. I guess we've been working too hard on the cookies. We snapped."

But the home ec teacher still looked furious.

"What cookies?" she demanded. "I don't even see any cookies." She turned to Jessica. "Are you going to have four hundred cookies ready for the TV show tomorrow?"

Jessica cleared her throat. "Sure. Yeah. Of course we are." At that moment, she would have said anything to escape Mrs. Gerhart's steely glare.

Mrs. Gerhart looked around the room, taking in the huge mess and the frazzled Unicorns, and finally catching sight of the repulsive-looking cookies.

"You don't look ready," she said icily. "I must say, if I had known it would turn out like this, I never would have recommended you to my friend Antoinette Maresca. I'm very sorry I got involved at all."

Jessica stared at her feet, feeling, if possible, even worse than she had before.

"I will be very upset indeed if you let my friend down," Mrs. Gerhart said grimly. "And I hate to think what will happen to your grade if you do."

Tears sprang into Jessica's eyes. Not her beloved honor roll status! She couldn't lose that!

"You all have fifteen minutes before the homeroom bell rings," Mrs. Gerhart said after checking her watch. "I suggest you start cleaning up this mess. It goes without saying that you're banned from this room in the future, except during regular class times. Also, I expect each of you to write a two-page essay explaining your deplorable behavior today. I want those essays on my desk by noon on Wednesday. I will choose the best essay and ask for it to be published in the *Sixers,* as an example to other students. Are there any questions?"

The Unicorns looked at one another sheepishly, then Tamara raised her hand. "Excuse me," she said timidly, "but I'm not sure we can finish cleaning up in here before homeroom."

"Then I will expect you back during lunchtime, your study halls, and after school, if necessary. This room will be spick-and-span by tomorrow morning or there will be grave consequences. Do I make myself clear?"

Jessica nodded meekly.

"Yes, ma'am," Mary said quietly.

Mrs. Gerhart turned and left the room.

Jessica stared at the cookie-dough-littered floor. She felt too terrible to look up. She was totally in disgrace, her cookies were a sticky, unending nightmare, and on top of everything else, she had to write a two-page essay about what a loser she was. With her luck, it would be the one chosen for publication in the *Sixers*. Jessica sniffled.

"OK, Unicorns," Janet said briskly. "Let's get going. We only have a few minutes."

Jessica heard bowls and utensils being picked up and loaded into the dishwasher.

"This stinks," Tamara muttered.

Someone started scraping cookies into the disposal.

"This just isn't worth it," Mary said bitterly.

Suddenly Janet thrust a large wet sponge into Jessica's hand.

"You too," Janet said coolly. "You can't just stand around."

Wordlessly, Jessica started wiping the countertops.

"I can't believe this," Belinda muttered as she sponged raw egg off the floor. "Look at me. I have to go through the rest of the day like this without changing." She gestured to her purple striped T-shirt and black jeans, which were covered with drying, stiffening batter.

"We're all a mess," Kimberly said testily as she put away their ingredients. "And after we've all worked so hard, too. And for what? Nothing."

"You can say that again," Ellen said fiercely. "And you know what? I don't care if I *am* a Unicorn. I'm bailing out on this whole thing, right now."

Jessica's eyes widened. "But—"

"Me, too," Mandy said.

Jessica's chest tightened. *Not now. Don't bail out on me now.*

Janet turned around from the dishwasher to stare at the Unicorns intently. "Look, I guess we should take a vote. We're all pretty unhappy and fed up. And it really looks like these cookies could ruin the Unicorn reputation forever. So . . . everyone who wants to leave the Unicookie business, say aye."

Eight loud ayes filled the air.

"You're on your own, Jessica," Janet announced, bending down to load the dishwasher.

Jessica gave the counter an angry swipe. She pushed her hair back roughly. *I can't believe they're dumping me,* she thought. *It's like they're putting me on an ice floe and setting me adrift.* Suddenly she felt almost close to tears.

"This means no TV show," Jessica reminded them, trying to keep her voice calm.

"Aye!" they all yelled.

"No glory for the Unicorns," Jessica said, scrubbing her counter furiously.

"Aye! Aye! Aye!"

Jessica stuck out her bottom lip and narrowed her eyes. "If I make the cookies by myself," she warned them, "they won't be called Unicookies. They'll be named after me."

"Aaayyyyyyyeeeeeeee!"

"Fine." Jessica rinsed her sponge and started on a new countertop. Those Benedict Arnolds. She would show them. They would be sorry. Somehow she would make them sorry. Somehow.

At lunchtime that day, Lila waited impatiently by the pay phone in the hallway outside the cafeteria. She was due in the home ec room to help clean, but she had a little job to do first.

Finally, the phone was free. Lila pulled the catalogue out from her backpack and punched a million numbers into the phone, ending with her credit-card number. She got through to the Gourmet Food from Switzerland customer service right away.

"Hello?" Lila said. "I just received your sugar-cookie sampler this morning, after I ordered it last weekend? Now I need to order thirty-four dozen of cookie number eight. Yes, the frosted sugar cookie in animal shapes."

It had been the closest thing to a Unicookie Lila had found. The Unicorns might have deserted Jessica, but Lila had something else up her sleeve. She pictured Jessica showing up empty-handed, humiliated, a failure, at the TV station. Then Lila would waltz in with platters full of "Unicookies." So what if they were from a gourmet store? Who would know? How many people in Sweet Valley ate cookies from Switzerland? Lila would save the day—not only for Jessica but for the Unicorns, and for herself. She would be interviewed on *Lifestyles of the French and Famous*. Jessica would owe her favors for the rest of her life. And Lila would be in a great position within the Unicorn club. For example, when they needed to elect a new president.

"Yes, I said thirty-four dozen," Lila said. "And I need them Federal Expressed to my house no later than eight o'clock tomorrow morning. Yeah, so? I know it's expensive. What's your point?" Lila tapped her foot. "OK, then. Make sure they're at my house no later than eight tomorrow morning, or heads will roll. Yeah. OK. Thanks. Bye." With a sly smile of triumph, Lila hung up the phone. This was the best plan she had ever had.

"So you got the home ec room cleaned?" Elizabeth asked timidly that afternoon. She and a silent, depressed Jessica were walking home together after school. "You didn't have to stay late?"

Jessica shook her head. "I finished up during my late study hall," she said in a low, sad voice.

"Cheer up, Jess," Elizabeth said, feeling her heart go out to her sister. "At least you were able to shower after P.E. Your hair looks totally normal now."

"It doesn't matter," Jessica sighed. "Nothing matters anymore. I'm hopeless. Tomorrow morning I have to call Antoinette Maresca, the producer of *Lifestyles of the French and Famous,* and tell her that me and my stupid cookies won't be coming after all. Then I have to write a two-page essay about how it feels to be on the road to failuredom. The Unicorns hate me, Mrs. Gerhart hates me, and I'm probably going to be blasted off the honor roll, after only one day of being on it. I'm a lost cause." Her voice broke a little bit.

Elizabeth's forehead wrinkled in concern. She hadn't seen Jessica so totally down since the last Johnny Buck concert had been canceled. But how could she cheer Jessica up? She herself was feeling a little low, too. Just that morning she had actually missed a word on a spelling quiz: serendipity. She had put in two p's. The principal's list was sliding further and further out of reach all the time. Elizabeth sighed. Serendipity. She would sure never miss it again. Now it was burned into her memory forever. Serendipity. Serendipity.

Jessica shuffled her feet glumly up the walkway to their house.

Poor Jessica, Elizabeth thought. *I wish I could help her somehow. Sure, she's let her fame go to her head a little bit, but I hate to see her like this. After all, she is my only twin sister.*

Serendipity . . .

Suddenly Elizabeth froze, her house key still in the lock.

She gasped, staring at Jessica. Jessica raised sad, hound dog eyes to her sister.

"What?" Jessica asked.

"Serendipity!" Elizabeth cried. "Do you know what it means?"

Jessica rolled her eyes. "That's right, Lizzie. Quiz me on vocabulary when I'm at my absolute lowest."

"No, no, you don't get it," Elizabeth said excitedly. "Serendipity! Come on! I have an idea." She flung open the front door and practically dragged Jessica back to the kitchen.

Ten

"Elizabeth, I appreciate what you're doing, but please, just give it up," Jessica moaned from where she sat at the kitchen table. "The Unicorns have already tried every single combination known to man. It won't work."

"Quit being so negative," Elizabeth said, quickly getting out flour, butter, sugar, eggs, and everything else she would need for her experiment. "You can't give up now. Don't you want to be on TV?"

"Yeah, of course I do, but not if it means making a total fool out of myself," Jessica responded.

With her practiced reporter's eye, Elizabeth tried to line up everything on the counter just the way it had been in home ec class last week, when she and Jessica had been so angry at each other. She got out all her mother's flavorings and lined them up. She couldn't remember exactly what had been there, or in what order, but she crossed her fingers and hoped for serendipity to take over.

"Come on, Jessica," Elizabeth urged. "We've made good cookies before. We can do it again. Let's just try one more thing, and then you can give up if you want to."

Grumbling, Jessica came over to the counter. "I hate cookies," she said. "I'll never eat another cookie as long as I live. I don't ever want to mix another batch of cookie dough in my whole life."

"Come on, now," Elizabeth said. "Quit being such a grumpus. You start sifting flour, while I measure the other stuff. And hurry up—we want to get this done and cleaned up before Mom gets back."

Jessica sullenly measured out the flour and began to sift it into a bowl. "It's not like you know cookies better than I do," she said sulkily. "After the last week, I know cookies better than anyone."

"Yeah, yeah," Elizabeth said, pretending to seem a little irritated. "The great Jessica Wakefield always knows best."

Jessica frowned as she sifted flour. "I didn't say that. I just said that I know how to make cookies."

"Uh-huh," Elizabeth said in an annoying tone that was calculated to drive Jessica up the wall. "Which is why you're so prepared to go on TV tomorrow. I get it."

She could feel Jessica start to seethe beside her. Praying that her plan would work, Elizabeth quickly bent down, pretending to pick up a spoon she had dropped.

"Look," Jessica said angrily, swinging around to confront Elizabeth. Sure enough, just as she had last Tuesday, she flung a cupful of sugar all over Elizabeth's shirt.

Elizabeth made her face look angry. "Jessica!" she cried. "Look what you've done!"

"I didn't mean to," Jessica protested. She reached out to brush the flour off, but just ended up smearing butter and raw egg over Elizabeth's front, exactly as she had last Tuesday.

"Quit it, you klutz!" Elizabeth snapped, hoping beyond hope that Jessica would go for the wooden spoon. Yes! She did! Elizabeth mentally punched the air with one fist.

"You quit it," Jessica snarled, waving her wooden spoon. "There you go again, acting all bossy. Just because you're four minutes older than me doesn't mean you always know best!"

Elizabeth frowned fiercely and stood close to Jessica, forcing her to back up next to the counter. "Oh, yeah?"

"Yeah!" Jessica cried, waving her spoon threateningly. Then, as Elizabeth watched in amazement, Jessica did the exact same thing she had done before: she knocked a bunch of different flavorings into her batter.

Staring down at her batter, Jessica shrieked. "Now look what you made me do! Another batch ruined!" She reached out to knock the flavorings away, but Elizabeth grabbed her hand.

"Hold it! Let's look at what's in there." Excitedly Elizabeth carefully picked out a small bottle of vanilla extract, a small bottle of almond extract, and a small plastic bag full of ground almond powder.

"OK, now," Elizabeth said breathlessly, grabbing the notebook and pen she had ready. "Don't move. Don't even breathe until I write this all down."

* * *

Ten minutes later the cookie sheets were in the oven.

"You see?" Elizabeth asked. "What we had to do was re-create the exact same situation as when you made those awesome cookies. It wasn't enough that you were in the home ec room this morning. *I* wasn't there, and we weren't arguing. You needed to duplicate the experiment exactly."

"I can't believe you did all that on purpose," Jessica said, shaking her head. "I was getting ready to brain you with my wooden spoon."

Elizabeth grinned. "Good thing you didn't. You never would have tried one extra teaspoon of vanilla, about one-half teaspoon almond extract, and about one-third cup of ground almonds."

Jessica gazed at her sister appreciatively. "I can't believe you went to so much trouble just for me—re-creating the argument and everything. You're better than all the Unicorns in the world."

"Don't thank me yet," Elizabeth said, holding up her hand. "Let's just see if it works." But deep inside, Elizabeth felt a thrill of anticipation. She had a feeling that these were the cookies. Already they smelled amazingly yummy, just baking. She and Jessica sat across from each other at the kitchen table, their fingers crossed.

When the timer went off, they ran to the oven and pulled out the cookie sheets. Setting them on the counter, the twins examined them closely.

Jessica looked up at Elizabeth and took a deep breath.

"They look like the cookies," she whispered. The cookies were a smooth, even shade of pale lavender.

"They smell like the cookies," Elizabeth whispered back. They smelled delicious, with hints of vanilla and almond wafting through the air.

"You try them," Jessica said. "They were your idea."

Elizabeth shook her head. "No. This is your baby."

Holding her breath, Jessica pried one up with a spatula, blew on it, and took a bite.

"Ow," she said, her mouth full. "Hot."

"Well? Well?" Elizabeth demanded, hopping around Jessica anxiously. "How is it?"

Jessica swallowed, then looked at Elizabeth. Her face split into an enormous smile that lit up the whole kitchen.

"It's fabulous!" she screamed, starting to jump up and down. "It's delicious! It's the best cookie in the whole world!"

Laughing hysterically, the twins grabbed each other's hands and danced around the kitchen together, not caring if they bumped into tables or chairs or cupboards or counters. They had found the recipe! Jessica's troubles were over.

"And then Elizabeth had this brilliant idea," Jessica said excitedly at dinner that night. She didn't mind giving Elizabeth credit. Even though it was Jessica's recipe, Elizabeth had saved the day, and Jessica wasn't going to forget it.

"So now we know exactly what's in Jessica's

cookies," Elizabeth finished, taking some chicken pie and putting it on her plate.

"That's great," Mrs. Wakefield said, smiling at her daughters. "So what happens next?"

"Next?" Jessica said in surprise. Her brows creased in concern. "Oh, gee. Next. Oh, sheesh." For a moment, she sat numbly in her chair, looking dismayed. "Well, I guess . . . I guess that's the thing," she went on in distress. "I can only be on *Lifestyles of the French and Famous* if I bring four hundred cookies for the studio audience."

"And when do you have to have them?" Mr. Wakefield asked.

"Tomorrow afternoon," Jessica groaned. "Right after school. I have to be at the TV studio at three thirty."

"*How* many cookies did you say you have to make?" Mrs. Wakefield asked.

"Four hundred," Jessica moaned, putting her head in her hands.

Steven snorted. "Kiss it good-bye," he said breezily, helping himself to another roll. "There's no way."

"Steven," Mr. Wakefield cautioned him. Then he turned to Jessica. "I think if we come up with some family teamwork, we might be able to get it done," he said. He looked at his wife. "What do you say, Alice?"

Mrs. Wakefield grinned. "I was about to say the same thing. Let me just finish my dinner and then I'll make a big cookie-ingredient run to the grocery store."

Jessica squealed with happiness and jumped up to hug her parents. Who needed the Unicorns, anyway?

"OK," Mr. Wakefield said, tying on his Kiss the Cook barbecue apron. "Let's get an assembly line going. Alice, you measure ingredients. Jessica, you sift the dry ingredients together. I'll cream the butter and the sugar. Elizabeth, you drop cookie dough onto cookie sheets. Since your mom bought some extra sheets, I think we can have three in the oven at the same time, and three ready to go with the next batch. Steven?"

Steven, who was slinking out the kitchen door toward the family room, looked cautiously over his shoulder. "Huh?"

"You can rotate the cookie sheets in the oven, scoop the baked cookies off the sheets, transfer them to the cooling racks, and then rinse the sheets for Elizabeth."

"Me?" Steven squeaked. "But there's a baseball game on."

"This is a family project," Mrs. Wakefield said firmly. "And you're part of this family."

"Hard to believe sometimes," Elizabeth muttered under her breath.

"Here." Mr. Wakefield handed Steven an apron, an oven mitt, and a spatula. "Let's go, son."

"Look, I've tasted their cookies," Steven said. "Believe me, you don't want to get involved."

"For your information, these are different cookies," Jessica told him indignantly.

Mr. Wakefield pointed silently to Steven's position in the assembly line.

Groaning, Steven went to stand next to the oven, ready to start shifting cookie sheets.

"What time is it?" Elizabeth asked groggily, covering a huge yawn with her hand.

"Almost two o'clock," Mrs. Wakefield answered, brushing a stray strand of blond hair behind her ear. She leaned weakly against the counter.

Steven was curled up beneath the kitchen table, snoring quietly.

Over by Steven, Jessica was counting cookies in a mindless drone. "Three hundred and ninety-one, three hundred and ninety-two," she muttered.

Mr. Wakefield was propped against the sink, his chin on his hands, his eyes closed. His apron was white with flour and speckled with bits of butter, raw dough, and egg.

Elizabeth scraped the last five cookies off the very last cookie sheet and brought them over to Jessica, almost stumbling over Steven's ankle as she did.

"Three hundred ninety-seven, three hundred ninety-eight . . ." Jessica's eyes were glazed over, and they didn't even flicker as Elizabeth dropped the last five cookies onto the cooling rack. The kitchen table was covered with every piece of Tupperware Mrs. Wakefield owned, as well as two roasting pans and a large cake tin. They were all packed with pale lavender cookies, sprinkled with powdered sugar.

Jessica numbly counted the last cookies. "Four hundred and three, four hundred and four." She looked up dully. "Any more?"

Elizabeth shook her head and collapsed into a chair. "That's it. That's everything."

Sighing, Jessica collapsed next to her. "We have four hundred and four cookies," she announced, a tiny smile crossing her batter-streaked face.

"Yay," Mrs. Wakefield said weakly. She, too, came to sit down, and Mr. Wakefield trudged over and sat next to her. The four of them sat around the kitchen table, looking at one another with exhausted satisfaction. Beneath their feet, Steven slept contentedly.

"I want to thank everyone," Jessica said, her head flopped back against her chair. "You're the best family ever. I couldn't have done it without you."

Mrs. Wakefield leaned over and scraped a dried piece of batter off Jessica's cheek. "We were glad to help, honey. That's what families are for."

Jessica idly examined the ends of her hair for any stray pieces of butter. "Well, you all saved my life. Especially Elizabeth." She smiled across at her sister. Elizabeth's eyes were half closed, and she was propped up on her hands. "It was all Elizabeth's idea. And I want you to come on TV tomorrow and meet Chef Crêpe with me."

Elizabeth opened her eyes and sat up a little, looking pleased. "Me? Really?"

"Of course," Jessica said. "I've even thought of a new name for the cookies: JEMS. The J is for me, and the E is for you."

"What's the M for?" Elizabeth asked.

Frowning, Jessica said, "I don't know, really. It just sounded good."

"Maybe the M is an upside-down W for Wakefield," their mother suggested.

"Yeah!" Jessica's face lit up. "That's what it is."

She looked around the table at all the cookies in all their containers. "Last week, I had these fancy boxes all planned," she said. "All white and purple, with my name on them in big purple letters. But now I'm just glad we're done. And hey!" she reached for a plate of cookies. "We have four hundred and four—which means there's one extra for each of us."

Mr. Wakefield looked at the cookies in alarm. "Oh, no, thanks," he said quickly. "I think I'll pass."

"You can have mine," Mrs. Wakefield offered.

"I don't want it," Elizabeth said bluntly.

Jessica giggled. "I guess I don't want mine either," she admitted. "But I think I know who will." She looked down at the sleeping form of her brother. He twitched in his sleep and paddled one arm, like a dog.

"Steven!" the Wakefields chorused.

Eleven

Early on Tuesday morning, the doorbell rang at Lila's house.

"I'll get it," she yelled, pounding down the steps before Mrs. Purvis could answer the front door.

It was the Federal Express man, and Lila eagerly signed for the eight large boxes from the Gourmet Foods from Switzerland company. Then she took all the boxes into the kitchen, where she had her supplies ready.

After ripping open the boxes and examining the cookies, Lila decided they were perfect. They definitely looked as if they could be called Unicookies. True, they weren't purple, but they were sugar cookies, and they were iced with white icing. They would definitely do.

She would get them all ready to go now, and then after school she would race home and have the Fowlers' chauffeur drive her to the TV station. Then she would simply waltz onto the set with her cookies. It was a no-fail plan: If Jessica hadn't shown up, Lila could say that *she* was Jessica, or that Jessica had sent her. Then Chef Crêpe would interview Lila alone. If Jessica was there, whether with disgusting cookies or with no cookies at all, she would still be thrilled to see Lila and would welcome her and her Swiss cookies with open arms. Then Lila could still be interviewed. No matter what happened, Lila was going to be looking pretty good by the end of the day.

After a quick glance at the clock, Lila lined up all the large trays that Mrs. Purvis usually used for their parties and hurriedly began arranging cookies on them. She couldn't help chuckling to herself. This was the most brilliant thing she had ever thought up. Wait till the Unicorns saw her on TV this afternoon. Thank heavens for good old Fowler ingenuity.

"So, Jessica," Lila said, taking a sip of milk. "What are your plans for this afternoon? What are you going to tell the people at *Lifestyles of the French and Famous*?" She studied her friend across the table. Jessica looked beat—totally pale, tired, and worn out. It was a good sign.

Ellen and Mary exchanged glances. Mandy, Belinda, and Janet all leaned closer to hear.

Jessica shrugged and pushed her fruit cocktail around in its compartment on her tray. "I don't know. I haven't planned anything. I guess I'll just have to play it by ear."

Janet met Lila's eyes and raised her eyebrows.

"Jessica, you don't have the cookies," Janet said

pointedly. "What are you going to do? I hope you don't mention the Unicorns."

"Well, it'll be OK," Jessica said casually, taking a bite of her lunch.

Nerves of steel, Lila thought with reluctant admiration. Jessica didn't even look all that worried or upset. She must be so numb with dread that she was beyond feeling.

"I'm glad I'm out of it," Belinda murmured, taking a bite of apple.

"Me, too," said Tamara. "I wouldn't do that show now even if you hypnotized me."

It was all Lila could do not to wriggle in her chair in excitement. *Just a few more hours,* she thought, *and I'll be famous. I'll be Lila Fowler, of Unicookie fame.*

"I mean it, Jessica," Janet said firmly yet delicately. "Please don't mention the Unicorns. We're really sorry you're in this mess, and we really tried to help, but it just didn't work. I don't want the Unicorns dragged down by something that wasn't our fault, OK?"

Jessica shrugged, but she didn't look that bummed. "OK. I promise not to mention the Unicorns." She gave Janet a little smile.

"Thanks, Jessica." Janet breathed a sigh of relief. "Like I said, we're all sorry it didn't work out. But we practically killed ourselves trying to help. No one can say we didn't try."

Nodding, Jessica played with the food on her tray. "It's true—no one could say you didn't try," she said. "Anyway, Elizabeth said she would go with me."

Kimberly looked concerned. "Jessica, are you

sure you should go? Maybe you should just call them up . . ."

"That's OK," Jessica said, shrugging. "If I don't go, they'll have this big empty blank in the middle of their show. So I guess I'll just have to go through with it."

"Well, better you than me," Janet muttered, brushing her hands briskly together.

No, Lila thought smugly. *Better me than her.*

Mrs. Wakefield was waiting for Jessica and Elizabeth right in front of school as soon as the bell rang. The twins raced out of their classes and piled into the back of their mother's car.

"Hurry, Mom," Jessica pleaded. "I have to go home and try to salvage my face somehow. I've seen dishrags that look healthier than I do. And what if the guest star is someone totally hot—some new French rock star or something?"

Elizabeth laughed. "Better not get your hopes up, Jess. But I have to say, I feel pretty limp myself," she admitted, peering into the rearview mirror.

"That's because neither of you got much sleep last night," their mother reminded them. "But don't worry. Just change your clothes and brush your hair, and I'm sure they'll put makeup on you at the TV studio."

"Here! Right here!" Lila shrieked, banging on the glass separating her from her chauffeur. The Fowlers' limo pulled to a smooth stop at the curb near the rear entrance of the local TV station. Lila examined her appearance in her small purse mirror. Hair, check; lip gloss, check; cute purple jumper with white T-shirt, check.

"Shall I help you with the platters, Miss Lila?" the driver offered.

Lila shook her head firmly. "No, thanks. I want to take them in myself. If you could just get the door for me."

The chauffeur opened the car's rear door, and Lila stepped out. Her new clogs clunked loudly on the sidewalk. Throwing her purse over her shoulder, Lila reached in and slid the heavy trays toward her.

"Here, let me."

The driver picked up the trays and loaded them into Lila's outstretched arms. She almost staggered under the weight of the five heavy silver trays. But it was OK. This was her destiny: to carry these cookies into the TV studio and steal Jessica's thunder.

"OK, thanks," Lila said through gritted teeth. "You can go home now, and I'll call when I need you to pick me up."

"Are you sure, Miss Lila? Maybe I had better—"

"Look, it's all under control," Lila choked out. "You can take off."

"Very well, Miss Lila." The driver got back into the car, and seconds later the limo purred down the street.

Lila took a deep breath. The entrance to the studio was about two hundred feet away. Her arms were already killing her. Her purse was banging her hip annoyingly. But she could do it. She had to.

Hesitantly she took one step, and then another.

She could hardly see where she was going. Craning her neck to one side, she looked ahead as best she could. Very, very slowly, feeling as if her arms were breaking, she headed down the sidewalk.

"OK, kids, you look great." Tina, the makeup artist for *Lifestyles*, pulled back and reviewed her work.

Jessica caught Elizabeth's gaze in the mirror. "Wow," she said. "You look like you just woke up from nine hours' sleep."

Elizabeth grinned. "You look pretty bright-eyed and bushy-tailed yourself."

"Tina, maybe after the show, could you explain what you did with the eyeliner?" Jessica asked, peering at herself in the mirror. "My eyes look humongous."

"Sure," Tina said with a smile. "Just come find me after the show."

A studio assistant holding a clipboard came into the makeup room. "Wakefields, let's go."

Elizabeth grinned at Jessica and gave her a thumbs-up sign. Jessica grinned back and squeezed her hand. Then they headed out into the cavernous TV set where *Lifestyles* was filmed. From the wings they could see their parents and Steven smiling excitedly in one of the front rows.

"OK, here are your cookies," the assistant told them, pointing to a fancy china platter where some cookies were arranged on linen napkins. "You'll carry these in to Chef Crêpe when it's your cue to go on."

"Jessica will carry the tray," Elizabeth said decisively.

"Then some of our gofers will start handing these other cookies out to the studio audience," the assistant continued.

"We don't have to do it?" Jessica asked.

He shook his head. "No. You'll be interviewed by Chef Crêpe. Remember some of the sample questions we went over?"

The twins nodded.

Jessica's heart was thundering with excitement. "Elizabeth," she said, turning to her sister, "two things: I just want to tell you how thankful I am that you're here to share this with me."

"Thanks," Elizabeth said. "I'm glad, too. What's the other thing?"

"Could you let me do most of the talking?"

"Wow! Whoa!" Lila staggered a little bit, feeling around with her clog for a solid footing. There had been a sudden three-inch dip in the curb that she hadn't seen, and for a few moments, her heavy trays had wavered precariously. But she had regained her balance and was edging closer to the studio door.

She could see it all now: herself smiling into the camera as Chef Crêpe interviewed her; Jessica looking grateful and ashamed at the same time, off-camera; the Unicorns, each watching TV in her own home, staring at Lila on the screen, feeling pea-green with jealousy.

"Yes, I call these Unicookies," Lila would say, looking modest. "They're the signature cookie of the Unicorn Club—you know, the club of the prettiest and most popular girls at Sweet Valley Middle School."

She practiced smiling into an invisible camera. And so on and so forth. It was going to be fabulous.

"How do I look?" Jessica whispered excitedly.

Elizabeth smiled. "You know you look great. That mini-dress was definitely the right choice."

"Thanks. You look great, too." Jessica grinned. "Chef Crêpe is getting two gorgeous blondes for the price of one."

Just then the studio assistant came up beside them again. "OK, you're on in two minutes. When I signal you, pick up your tray of cookies and walk over to that masking-tape X on the floor by Chef Crêpe. Got it?"

Jessica nodded confidently. "Got it."

"And when Jean Voilan comes out, just smile and shake his hand naturally. Then offer him a cookie."

"Jean Voilan!" Jessica gasped, putting her hand to her throat. "Is he the guest star? But he was on just last week!"

The assistant nodded. "He had a good time and wanted to come back. He and Chef Crêpe are going to make an asparagus soufflé."

"Oh, my gosh!" Jessica clutched Elizabeth's hand. "This is even better than I dreamed! Can you believe it? In a few minutes I'll be standing on the same stage as Jean Voilan!" She pressed a hand to her forehead. "I think I feel faint."

Elizabeth smiled wryly and rolled her eyes. "And who could blame you? After all, it's every girl's dream come true."

At that moment, the studio audience started clapping, then the assistant motioned for Jessica and Elizabeth to head onto the set. With a last, beaming smile at Elizabeth, Jessica picked up her tray, and they walked into the glare of the bright studio lights.

OK, Lila, just a few more feet. Keep going, girl. Your future waits behind that door. It was taking much longer than she had expected, and Lila wished for the thousandth time that she had asked the chauffeur to stay to help her.

Sweat had dampened her long brown hair and it was sticking to her forehead. She knew her face must be flushed and her touch of mascara ruined. But she could repair that inside. Her arms were trembling, her legs felt weak, and her new clogs were wearing a terrible blister on her left big toe.

It will all be worth it. I'm almost there. The studio door loomed ahead of her, at the top of a short ramp. Slowly, Lila maneuvered her way toward the ramp, then felt for the base with one foot. There! Now she started up the ramp, balancing her heavy trays, wishing she could see more, sick of the cookie smell that kept wafting up into her face.

Finally, she made it up the ramp. "Oh, no!" she groaned, realizing she had no way of opening the door. Just as she was deciding to kick on the door until someone opened it for her, someone did.

The large metal door swung out suddenly. Lila was standing much too close, and the man barreled into her and her five trays of cookies.

"Aiieeee!" Lila screamed, tottering backward, trying desperately to juggle her cookies.

"Oh! Sorry, miss!" The man grabbed her arms to try to steady her, but it was no use. With an anguished, smothered shriek, Lila toppled backward down the ramp until she fell down hard on her behind on the grass. Her trays of cookies flew up into the air and then started landing on her head, one heavy *bonk* at a time. Cookies sprayed everywhere, like hundreds of tiny, iced, airborne missiles, and they too began to fall to the ground all around Lila. The heat had made the icing soften, and with too many damp little splats to count, Lila felt herself pelted with cookies.

"Oh, no," she moaned, thrusting the trays aside. Her butt hurt, and she thought she might have twisted an ankle. One clog was beneath her and the other was back on the ramp.

The man ran down the ramp toward her. "Miss, are you OK? Didn't you know that that door opened outward? Are you OK?"

"I don't know yet," Lila answered miserably, trying to brush the cookies off her. She looked around to see if there was any way she could save enough cookies to try to get on *Lifestyles*. It didn't look good. Most of them were broken, and some of them were dirty, lying on the ground. The icing was smeared, and the doilies were ruined.

"Gee, I'm really sorry," the man said. "Are you from catering?"

"No," Lila said with cold despair. "I'm a guest on *Lifestyles of the French and Famous*. The cookies were the special guest recipe."

Absentmindedly the man picked up part of a

cookie and popped it into his mouth. "Really? That's funny. How many kids with cookies are they going to have on that show? There's already a pair of twins in there. Chef Crêpe couldn't get enough of their cookies."

"What?" Lila shrieked. "They're already in there? Why didn't you tell me?" Scrambling to her feet, she tried to brush off as much cookie debris as possible. Of course, some was still sticking to her—all over her. The icing was impossible to get rid of. Stomping past the man, Lila shoved her other clog on, then yanked open the studio door and headed for the set of *Lifestyles*.

"Yes, Mademoiselle Jessica," Chef Crêpe was saying, "these cookies of yours are positively *magnifiques*. I salute and congratulate you."

"Thank you," Jessica said, beaming into a TV camera. "I guess some people just have a knack for baking. As you yourself said, Chef Crêpe, cooking is an art form. And as with any art, we have to rely on inspiration."

"Ah," Chef Crêpe continued. "So you feel that you were inspired to make such an amazing cookie?"

"I certainly do," Jessica said firmly. "Inspiration definitely played a huge part in the cookies' creation."

"That and serendipity," Elizabeth put in, leaning closer to Jessica.

Jessica frowned slightly. "Sarah nobody," she said indignantly. "These cookies are pure Jessica Wakefield, through and through!"

Among the studio audience, gofers were handing out cookies as fast as they could, and cautioning people to take only one each. When people started to sample the cookies, there were gasps of delight.

"Wow! Can I have another one?"

"These are incredible!"

"This has got to be the best cookie I've ever had."

"I've got to have another one! Please! Just one more."

Up on the set, Jessica and Elizabeth beamed.

"Ma'am?" a gofer asked Mrs. Wakefield, holding out a tray of cookies. "Care to sample a JEM?"

Mrs. Wakefield's face fell, and Mr. Wakefield looked panicky. Steven held up his hands in front of himself in the shape of a cross.

"Get away from me," he croaked.

"No, no, thank you," Mrs. Wakefield said quickly. "Someone else can have mine."

"Me, too," said the twins' father, looking pale.

On the set, Jessica and Elizabeth started laughing, and gave each other high fives. Neither of them saw Lila standing in the wings, close to tears and looking almost fuzzy with stuck-on cookie bits.

Twelve

"I'm thinking of trying something a little more ambitious," Jessica said in home ec class later that week, tossing her hair over her shoulder. "When I was on *Lifestyles of the French and Famous,* Jean Voilan and I were swapping recipes. Remember? He was on that day. With me. He had a stunning soufflé idea, but I think with a little inspiration I could probably improve on it." Breathing on her fingernails, she rubbed them on her white peasant blouse and then examined them casually.

Next to her, Elizabeth rolled her eyes, then winked at Amy Sutton. "I don't think we're going to be doing soufflés in here anytime soon, Jess," Elizabeth said, smothering her grin.

"Tut," Jessica said. "I know Mrs. Gerhart will let me skip ahead of the next couple of assignments. Why should I waste my time on a basic chicken casserole when culinary history is waiting to be made?"

"*What* kind of history?" Todd Wilkins asked,

wrinkling his nose. "Was that a dirty word, Jessica?"

His partner, Aaron Dallas, snorted in laughter, and even Elizabeth couldn't help giggling.

Jessica merely looked down her nose at them.

"*No*," she said. "Of course, Todd, I wouldn't expect you to understand, but it has to do with *cooking*. But you just stick to making soup from a can. Elizabeth," she continued, turning to her sister, "I'm thinking of concentrating mainly on desserts. Every great chef has a specialty, you know. I really think I could make a name for myself in desserts. What do you think of a chocolate mousse cake, sort of built in towers, with raspberry creme between the layers, and white chocolate icing, and the whole thing built up to about three feet tall?"

"Well, Jess"—Elizabeth raised her eyebrows—"maybe you should start with something a little less ambitious. After all, you're still recovering from the cookies episode. You don't want to strain yourself."

Jessica waved away her concerns. "You worry too much."

At that moment Mrs. Gerhart came in and held up a stack of papers. "Good morning, class," she said. "I have here your comparative shopping reports. Most of you did very well. Remember, these reports will count as ten percent of your final grade."

Jessica smiled confidently. She was sure she'd done well. After all, she was on the honor roll this month. It would practically be hard for her *not* to do well from now on. She would probably be on the honor roll every month from now till eighth-grade graduation. And the assignment hadn't been difficult. Some of it had been a *little* tricky, but Jessica thought she had come up with creative solutions to the problems.

Next to her, Elizabeth got her paper. As usual, she had gotten an A.

"Just an A," Elizabeth muttered. "Not an A+. Dang."

Jessica rolled her eyes. Today after school, she was really going to have to talk to Elizabeth about getting some sort of life. It seemed as if her sister did nothing but study nowadays.

Then Mrs. Gerhart handed her her own paper. Smiling, Jessica took it and looked for the grade. There it was, written in red ink at the top. Jessica gasped.

"But—" she sputtered. "But—"

"I'm sorry, Jessica," Mrs. Gerhart said patiently. "But you didn't really follow the instructions. It seems you just made up your own."

"But a D+!" Jessica whispered, horrified. "This will wreck my whole grade! This means I'll—" She stopped, realizing that beyond a doubt she would be booted off the honor roll. And she had been on it barely a week!

"I'm sorry, Jessica," Mrs. Gerhart said again. "I'll be willing to give you some sort of extra-credit assignment if you want to try to pull your grade up to a C or a B. And your two-page essay from last Wednesday was very nice. Come talk to me about it after class."

She headed off to finish handing out papers.

"I'm off the honor roll," Jessica said to Elizabeth. "I should have known it was too good to be true. Good thing Mom and Dad took us out to dinner *last* week."

"I'm really sorry, Jess," Elizabeth said, looking sympathetic. "I can help you with your extra-credit project, if you like."

Jessica sighed. "Yeah—maybe if I did some sort of special cooking project . . ." She frowned. "You know, in some ways, being on the honor roll is unnatural for me. I mean, I can't remember the last time Lila and I watched a movie together over the phone. I haven't even had time to go to Casey's. No, I think maybe I'll just let things stay as they are—go back to being the old Jessica. After all," she said, straightening up, "there's more to life than being on the honor roll. There's still my cooking career."

"That's true," Elizabeth said, smiling at her.

"So, Elizabeth," Mr. Bowman said that afternoon right before their *Sixers* meeting started. "Do we run this article about Jessica or not?"

"Maybe we still should," Elizabeth said thoughtfully. "I mean, she's already back off the honor roll for next month, but she did achieve a lot with her cookies. What do you think?"

Mr. Bowman shrugged. "It's OK with me, and you're the editor. I'll let it be your decision."

"You know, it's funny about Jessica," Elizabeth said. "She's off the honor roll, but it isn't really bothering her. I would be much more bummed if I weren't on the honor roll."

"That's because you're you, Elizabeth," Mr. Bowman said. "You're naturally more conscientious than Jessica. I remember your parents saying something like that to me at our last parent/teacher conference."

"Really? My parents noticed that?" Elizabeth was surprised.

Mr. Bowman laughed. "I think everyone's noticed it, Elizabeth. People who know you really appreciate your special qualities. I know I do."

Elizabeth smiled. She realized that she'd been feeling pretty unappreciated lately, with everyone making such a fuss over Jessica.

"So is Jessica bouncing back from her brief time in the spotlight?" the teacher asked.

Elizabeth grinned. "She's already totally forgotten that her cookies were made by serendipity. Last I heard, she's planning a career as a flashy star chef at some trendy restaurant. She always bounces back."

Mr. Bowman chuckled. "Does she know that her two-page essay about the home ec room disaster has been chosen to appear in this week's *Sixers*?"

"Not yet." Elizabeth laughed. "I haven't thought of a way to break it to her."

Then other *Sixers* staff members started to trickle in, and soon the meeting was underway, but somehow her conversation with Mr. Bowman kept replaying in Elizabeth's mind.

Jessica's bounced back, all right, but what about me? she wondered. *Am I going to bounce back?* Elizabeth hadn't had a moment's relaxation in what seemed like forever—she'd been too intent on getting better-than-perfect grades. Was it really worth it? What was she trying to prove? Maybe she could actually learn something from Jessica, as scary as that sounded. Maybe she should just be content to be who she was.

Of course, that's easy for me to say now, now that Jessica has sunk to her usual academic level, Elizabeth thought a little guiltily. Then she shook her head. This decision felt right to her, no matter what Jessica or anyone else was doing. Maybe in a month or two she could try again for the principal's list. But for right now, she was going to be just plain old honor roll Elizabeth. And this afternoon, she was going to make a point of doing something purely fun. Maybe she would get Jessica, and they would go to Casey's.

"Hmmm, excellent idea, Elizabeth." Jessica slurped her straw at the bottom of her strawberry milk shake.

"Yeah. A Casey's milk shake always cures what ails you," Elizabeth agreed. She wiped off her chocolate mustache with a napkin.

Sighing contentedly, Jessica leaned back against her seat. "It's been a pretty crazy couple of weeks," she said. "It'll be nice to have things back to normal for a little while."

Elizabeth's blue-green eyes widened. "Nice to have things back to normal?" She peered at Jessica suspiciously. "What have you done with the real Jessica?"

Jessica giggled and stuck out her tongue at her sister.

"Actually, I have a little news for you," Elizabeth said, scooping the very last bit of ice cream out of her milk shake glass. "Speaking of things not going back to normal."

"Um, you fell off the honor roll, too," Jessica guessed.

Elizabeth rolled her eyes. "Oh, I'm so sure. Actually—" She leaned forward conspiratorially. "Mom just told me before we left the house. Guess who's coming to visit for two solid weeks?"

Jessica thought for a minute. Then her face lit up. "Johnny Buck? Maybe he's coming to Sweet Valley to relax for a while."

"Jessica!" Elizabeth groaned. "Get real. No, this is someone you know personally."

"Do I like them?" Jessica frowned.

"You like *her* very much. You love having her come visit," Elizabeth confirmed.

"I give up," Jessica said finally.

"Cousin Robin from San Diego," Elizabeth announced triumphantly.

"You're kidding!" Jessica shrieked. "Really?"

Elizabeth nodded happily. "Yep. Her parents are going to Europe for two weeks to celebrate their fifteenth wedding anniversary. So Robin's coming to stay with us for the entire time. And Mom says that she's going to go to school with us and everything."

"Way cool," Jessica said, looking excited. "It'll be so much fun to have her here. We can take her to the mall, she can hang out with the Unicorns—maybe we could even have a party for her or something."

"Yeah. We'll have to think of lots of really fun things to do when Robin's here," Elizabeth agreed. "I bet her visit is going to be the most fun ever."

Will Robin's visit be the most fun ever? Or will Elizabeth find that two's company and three's a crowd? Read Sweet Valley Twins #90,* THE COUSIN WAR, *to find out.

Bantam Books in the SWEET VALLEY TWINS series.
Ask your bookseller for the books you have missed.

#1 BEST FRIENDS
#2 TEACHER'S PET
#3 THE HAUNTED HOUSE
#4 CHOOSING SIDES
#5 SNEAKING OUT
#6 THE NEW GIRL
#7 THREE'S A CROWD
#8 FIRST PLACE
#9 AGAINST THE RULES
#10 ONE OF THE GANG
#11 BURIED TREASURE
#12 KEEPING SECRETS
#13 STRETCHING THE TRUTH
#14 TUG OF WAR
#15 THE OLDER BOY
#16 SECOND BEST
#17 BOYS AGAINST GIRLS
#18 CENTER OF ATTENTION
#19 THE BULLY
#20 PLAYING HOOKY
#21 LEFT BEHIND
#22 OUT OF PLACE
#23 CLAIM TO FAME
#24 JUMPING TO CONCLUSIONS
#25 STANDING OUT
#26 TAKING CHARGE
#27 TEAMWORK
#28 APRIL FOOL!
#29 JESSICA AND THE BRAT ATTACK
#30 PRINCESS ELIZABETH
#31 JESSICA'S BAD IDEA
#32 JESSICA ON STAGE
#33 ELIZABETH'S NEW HERO
#34 JESSICA, THE ROCK STAR
#35 AMY'S PEN PAL
#36 MARY IS MISSING
#37 THE WAR BETWEEN THE TWINS
#38 LOIS STRIKES BACK
#39 JESSICA AND THE MONEY MIX-UP
#40 DANNY MEANS TROUBLE
#41 THE TWINS GET CAUGHT
#42 JESSICA'S SECRET
#43 ELIZABETH'S FIRST KISS
#44 AMY MOVES IN

Sweet Valley Twins Super Editions

#1 THE CLASS TRIP
#2 HOLIDAY MISCHIEF
#3 THE BIG CAMP SECRET
#4 THE UNICORNS GO HAWAIIAN
#5 LILA'S SECRET VALENTINE

Sweet Valley Twins Super Chiller Editions

#1 THE CHRISTMAS GHOST
#2 THE GHOST IN THE GRAVEYARD
#3 THE CARNIVAL GHOST
#4 THE GHOST IN THE BELL TOWER
#5 THE CURSE OF THE RUBY NECKLACE
#6 THE CURSE OF THE GOLDEN HEART
#7 THE HAUNTED BURIAL GROUND
#8 THE SECRET OF THE MAGIC PEN

Sweet Valley Twins Magna Editions

THE MAGIC CHRISTMAS
BIG FOR CHRISTMAS
A CHRISTMAS WITHOUT ELIZABETH

#45 LUCY TAKES THE REINS
#46 MADEMOISELLE JESSICA
#47 JESSICA'S NEW LOOK
#48 MANDY MILLER FIGHTS BACK
#49 THE TWINS' LITTLE SISTER
#50 JESSICA AND THE SECRET STAR
#51 ELIZABETH THE IMPOSSIBLE
#52 BOOSTER BOYCOTT
#53 THE SLIME THAT ATE SWEET VALLEY
#54 THE BIG PARTY WEEKEND
#55 BROOKE AND HER ROCK-STAR MOM
#56 THE WAKEFIELDS STRIKE IT RICH
#57 BIG BROTHER'S IN LOVE!
#58 ELIZABETH AND THE ORPHANS
#59 BARNYARD BATTLE
#60 CIAO, SWEET VALLEY!
#61 JESSICA THE NERD
#62 SARAH'S DAD AND SOPHIA'S MOM
#63 POOR LILA!
#64 THE CHARM SCHOOL MYSTERY
#65 PATTY'S LAST DANCE
#66 THE GREAT BOYFRIEND SWITCH
#67 JESSICA THE THIEF
#68 THE MIDDLE SCHOOL GETS MARRIED
#69 WON'T SOMEONE HELP ANNA?
#70 PSYCHIC SISTERS
#71 JESSICA SAVES THE TREES
#72 THE LOVE POTION
#73 LILA'S MUSIC VIDEO
#74 ELIZABETH THE HERO
#75 JESSICA AND THE EARTHQUAKE
#76 YOURS FOR A DAY
#77 TODD RUNS AWAY
#78 STEVEN THE ZOMBIE
#79 JESSICA'S BLIND DATE
#80 THE GOSSIP WAR
#81 ROBBERY AT THE MALL
#82 STEVEN'S ENEMY
#83 AMY'S SECRET SISTER
#84 ROMEO AND 2 JULIETS
#85 ELIZABETH THE SEVENTH-GRADER
#86 IT CAN'T HAPPEN HERE
#87 THE MOTHER-DAUGHTER SWITCH
#88 STEVEN GETS EVEN
#89 JESSICA'S COOKIE DISASTER